HIDING OUT AT THE Pancake PALACE

NAN MARINO

ROARING BROOK PRESS NEW YORK

For my sister Jane
and
for my friends at Toms River Info Services:
Thanks for making me feel at home in New Jersey.

Excerpt from "The Air Tune" from *The Pine Barrens* by John McPhee. Copyright © 1967, 1968 by John McPhee. Reprinted with permission of Farrar, Straus and Giroux, LLC.

Text copyright © 2013 by Nan Marino
Illustrations copyright © 2013 by John Hendrix
Published by Roaring Brook Press
Roaring Brook Press is a division of Holtzbrinck Publishing Holdings
    Limited Partnership
175 Fifth Avenue, New York, New York 10010
mackids.com

Library of Congress Cataloging-in-Publication Data
Marino, Nan.
    Hiding out at the Pancake Palace / Nan Marino. — 1st ed.
        p.   cm.
    Summary: "When musical prodigy Elvis Ruby completely freezes up on television, he is forced to hide out in the Pinelands of New Jersey and try to find his way back to the music once again with the help of a new friend" — Provided by publisher.
        ISBN 978-1-59643-753-1 (hardback)
        ISBN 978-1-59643-859-0 (ebook)
        [1. Singers—Fiction.   2. Musicians—Fiction.   3. Fame—Fiction.   4. Friendship—Fiction.   5. Gifted children—Fiction.   6. Stage fright—Fiction.   7. Pine Barrens (N.J.)—Fiction.]   I. Title.
    PZ7.M33885Hid 2013
    [Fic]—dc23
                                                                        2012021601

Roaring Brook Press books are available for special promotions and premiums. For details contact: Director of Special Markets, Holtzbrinck Publishers.

First edition 2013
Book design by Andrew Arnold
Printed in the United States of America by RR Donnelley & Sons Company,
    Harrisonburg, Virginia

10   9   8   7   6   5   4   3   2

"Music is perpetual, and only hearing is intermittent."
—Henry David Thoreau

"No one, of course, knows how it goes, but the Air Tune is there, everywhere, just beyond hearing."
—John McPhee, *The Pine Barrens*

Where the Hiders Go

If you need somewhere to hide, try the Pinelands of New Jersey.

It's a wild place filled with swamp streams. And sand hills. Salt marshes and bogs. There are towns too, some so small they don't make it on the map. No one pays attention to them anyway.

For a hider, that is the beauty of the Pinelands. The entire place can go unnoticed. The trees are stubby, the paths are hard to find, and the streams are lazy and slow. Nothing about it stands out. People drive by on their way to somewhere else.

For a hider, this is good. It makes it easier to slip away.

A place like this you can trust with your secrets.

A place like this has secrets of its own.

And here's the first.

They say that when the trees get restless they sing.

But it's the Pinelands, so most people don't notice that either.

The Perils of Happiness

The night the hider came to town, Cecilia Wreel decided to sneak out of her bedroom window. She was not quite eleven and it was her first time climbing out at night.

Cecilia slipped out of bed, grabbed her eyeglasses, and put on her pink bunny slippers while Storm, her miniature dachshund, begged and pleaded to go. He cried and whined and looked like a flying hotdog when he jumped into the air.

Before she could quiet him down, there was a knock on the bedroom door. "Everything okay in there?"

It was her mother.

Cecilia dove under the covers, bunny slippers and all. The door creaked open. She could feel her mother's worried stare as she lay with her eyes closed, taking fake sleepy breaths.

"Are you awake?" her mother asked, almost hopeful. It took everything in Cecilia's power not to blurt out "Yes!" And all the while that her mother stood there watching, the urge to blurt grew greater. She was not a girl who was used to keeping secrets.

Later, much later, when the house was quiet, Cecilia tossed some crackers on the floor for Storm. It was a bribe for silence and Storm took it too. He lapped up every last crumb. But by the time Cecilia got halfway out the window, Storm was whining again. "I'll be back soon," she whispered, which made him whimper even more.

Cecilia climbed down into the Pinelands night. She expected to see starlight and moonlight, but the clouds had come in quick and her flashlight was dim. As soon as her feet hit the path made of sugar sand, she broke into a run.

Don't let the sweet name fool you. Sugar sand is so fine and powdery that it can grab hold of something and not let go. When you walk in it, you sink in deep. And if you're careless enough to run, you're bound to lose a bunny slipper or two.

The first one flopped off before Cecilia even made it through her own back yard, somewhere between the goldfish pond and the old shed. She hopped around on one foot searching for it. That's how she lost the second one.

Barefoot, she doubled back and retraced her steps. She

crouched down on her hands and knees and sifted through the sand. Cecilia found the first one by the pond, its little bunny face staring solemnly at the water. With one slipper on, she limped toward the edge of the yard.

Cecilia stood where her parents' property ended and the woods began. She pointed her finger at the trees and gave them her command. "Sing."

A few of the more polite trees rustled. But most of them stood there, silent.

"Please." She was begging now. "A small song."

Cecilia pushed her glasses up her nose and pointed into the darkness with her flashlight. Somewhere inside those woods was the rugged bank of a cedar swamp stream where Cecilia had been born. It was a total accident. Her parents were out camping and she had surprised them by coming into the world a month early (and her mother always said it was the first surprise of many). Her father wrapped her in his flannel shirt, and her mother held her in her arms. And while her parents sat by the banks of the stream near the curly grass ferns, Cecilia put her fist into her mouth and tasted flannel.

That night, there was music in the pines. A real song, one with a melody, a harmony, and a beat. Her father said it was everywhere. Her mother said it started before Cecilia took her very first breath.

Cecilia had heard the story a hundred, no a thousand

times. Her parents told it over and over again. Her father liked to tell it at Cecilia's birthday dinners. Her mother whispered it to her the day Mr. Finn the goldfish died and again the day that Natalie Bracer said Cecilia's glasses were "too big for her face." No matter who told it and why and when, it always ended the same way.

"Those trees don't sing for everyone. That song played just for you."

For Cecilia that was the best part.

But earlier that evening when she had asked her parents to tell it again, the story had a different ending. The three of them were sitting on the porch swing that was only built for two. Storm had curled up on her lap.

Her father started. He told about the darkness of the cedar swamp and how they went too far into the woods to make it back to town. And how Cecilia's mother had shouted, "We need to figure out something quick. This baby's coming out now!"

Usually this was where her mother joined in. But tonight, she had been quiet. And when Cecilia asked about the music, her mother was quiet about that too.

Oblivious to her mother's silence, her father had continued. "That song was everywhere. Up in the trees. Down in the water. It felt as if the pines themselves were singing."

This was her mother's favorite part. She always added the

important details. The flannel shirt was a soft blue. The song was so loud it caused the stream to ripple. The flowers on the curly grass ferns looked like stars.

But tonight, there were no details shared.

The swing creaked back and forth before her mother spoke. "What if. What if. What if," she said over and over again.

"What if what?" demanded Cecilia.

"What's wrong, Stephanie?" her father asked.

Storm flicked his ears a bit and then went back to snoring.

There was an odd puffy sound when her mother exhaled, as if the breath she had just let out had been trapped inside her for years. "I've been thinking about it for a long time," she confessed. "What if it wasn't music? What if we didn't hear a song?" She waved at the pines in the back yard, which of course were silent. "Singing trees? How can that be?"

Wow. That was a clunker.

An ice-cold chunky clunker.

This was not how the story should go.

Her mother put her hand on Cecilia's shoulder. "I have a new theory," she announced. This was no big surprise. Her mother had theories for everything. "Remember how happy we were? How *extremely* happy we were back then?"

Her father nodded. "We were overjoyed. But what does this have to do with anything?"

"Well," said her mom, "I read in a magazine that extreme happiness causes your brain to produce this chemical called endorphins. And too much of it can cloud your reasoning." Her father tried to interrupt, but her mother held up her hand. "So maybe we were both so happy about the birth of our child that we *imagined* we heard music. Maybe we were *insanely* happy. And that's why we thought the trees sang."

Cecilia and her father protested at the same time.

"But, Mom" was all Cecilia could say.

Her father marched into the house. Cecilia and her mother followed.

"We weren't the first to hear music in the pines." Her father pulled a book off the shelf and he pointed to a page. "Over a hundred years ago, they say a fiddler named Sammy Buck heard it. He even learned to play it on the fiddle for his friends."

"Oh, I know the story of Sammy Buck," said her mom. "I grew up here too. I know all those old folktales. They're lovely old stories, but not exactly reliable."

"Folktales are often based in truth," said her dad. "Besides, others have heard it. My grandfather told me that when he was a boy playing hide-and-seek in the sand hills, notes rang out. Remember? He used to say it exactly that way. Notes rang out. Are you doubting the words of my grandfather?"

Her mother left the room. When she came back, she tossed a magazine on her husband's lap. "Here. Read this."

Cecilia's father held it, unopened, in his hands. "You're changing your mind because of something you read in *Celebrity Scoop Magazine*? This is a gossip magazine about rock stars and reality shows and movie people. Talk about your unreliable sources." He looked at the picture of a curly-haired boy on the cover and said, "I'm surprised you read this stuff."

"The health and fitness articles happen to be very good," said her mom. "That's the only part I read." She turned to Cecilia. "Sweetie, you're almost eleven. You're old enough to understand. We need to be logical. How could we really have heard a song?"

How long? How long ago did her mother change her mind? How long had she been keeping this secret?

Cecilia took a deep breath. It would be okay. Her father would make her mother remember and he would still tell the story on her birthdays and whenever Uncle Frank came. It would all go back to the way it was. To the way it *should* be.

But what if her father was already having doubts?

It could happen.

Then who knows? Maybe in a year or two, *both* parents would be sitting on that porch swing, wearing sheepish smiles, joking about the perils of happiness and how it can lead a person to imagine all kinds of crazy things. "Like singing trees." She could picture her father throwing his head back and laughing his deep laugh. She could almost hear her mother's soft chuckles.

Her song. The one that played just for her.

It would be gone.

And so there was only one logical thing to do.

And that was to sneak outside to the edge of the woods and wait for the trees to sing.

But when Cecilia stood, half barefoot, in front of the pines, they refused to cooperate. No matter how long she stood. No matter how quiet she was. No matter how many times she leaned into the darkness to listen.

Instead of music, she heard the sound of a car engine. Cecilia looked toward the road and saw headlights. It was odd to see a car on the road this time of night. With one slipper still missing, she limped to the front of the house.

The car was shiny, low to the ground, and sleek, not one she recognized. It stopped by the Hunt and Fishing Club. Then it inched forward a bit, moving on toward the Lost Treasures Thrift and Throwaway Store, then to Barnegat Al's Auto Repair, then to the old church. Obviously the driver was looking for something. Or someone.

Cecilia ducked underneath Cheryl McKenzie's blueberry stand, but she was not the type of person who could stay tucked inside a wooden box that said "Best Berries in Town" while something interesting and exciting was going on. She leaned out from her hiding place and peeked.

In the back seat, pressed up against the window, she saw a face. It was blurry, hard to make out. But Cecilia saw a pair of eyes. And the eyes saw her. She was sure of it.

The shiny car lurched forward, then it stopped in front of Piney Pete's, the only restaurant in town. But at this time of night, that was closed too.

The car door opened. A boy with long hair ran out, turned around, then ran back to the car. Or was it a girl? Cecilia was too far away to tell.

She hoped it was a girl.

But either way, this was a person who didn't want to be seen.

The Palace

The boy riding in the sleek shiny car was too busy staring at the sameness of the pine trees to notice Cecilia. At least, at first. But when he pressed his face against the window and glanced down at the blueberry stand, a pair of eyes behind very oversized glasses stared back at him.

He sank back into his seat. It had been a long day. He was extremely tired. He was imagining things. Besides no one wore eyeglasses that looked like that anymore.

The car heaved forward before he was able to take a second look.

His father was asking him a question, but the words blended together with the song that played on the radio. They turned into a driveway, and his father asked again, "Have you thought about a name? If you don't come up with a new name, people will recognize you."

The boy bolted out of the car as soon as it came to a complete stop, surprised that even after the long drive he still felt that urge to run. He took a few steps, first one way then the other.

He ran his hands through his long curly hair, like he always did when he felt jittery, and gave a hard look in the direction of the blueberry stand. But he saw nothing.

No eyes. No out-of-fashion oversized eyeglasses. Nothing. Good.

Nothing was good.

His little sister, Cher, stuck her head out the window. "What about Christopher? Or Luke is nice." Then she grinned. "Or how about Aaron?"

He liked that one.

"Are you sure you don't want us to stay with you?" his father asked.

"Aaron" shook his head. It would be impossible to hide all three of them. Besides, he was the only one they were looking for. "No. I'm fine." He smiled at Cher when he said it. She smiled back, then put her hand over her mouth, embarrassed by her missing front teeth.

"Dad," he heard Cher whisper. "Look at this place. Where are we anyway?"

"Wares Grove."

"Where's what?" Cher asked.

"Wares Grove. It's the name of the town. Wares Grove, New Jersey."

Cher poked her head out of the car again. "Hey, Aaron." She said his new name like it was the most natural thing in the world. Like she'd been calling him that every day for the past seven years of her life. "We're in New Jersey. And this"—she pointed to the trees around her—"is supposed to be a town."

It was hard to tell where they were or how far they had driven. He had spent the first part of the trip under blankets in the back seat. Plus, there had been evasive maneuvers that involved traveling south, north, east, and west on highways and side streets in case they were followed. The famous are always followed.

"Hey, Dad," Cher said, "I thought you said we were going to a palace."

Aaron stuck his head back into the car just in time to see his dad extend his hands and legs and lean into a good long stretch. No one stretched like his father. In cars, trains, buses, it didn't matter where he was, the man could outstretch a cat.

His father pointed to a painted sign near the roofline of a nearby cottage that said "Piney Pete's Pancake Palace."

A single porch light flickered on and off. There were no streetlights. The moonlight was dim. But even in the darkest, most shadowy depths of night, it was obvious. This was no palace. If you didn't count the barely visible spiderweb that hung like a curtain from the top of the front porch, the cottage was a tidy one. But "palace"?

"Are you kidding me?" Cher and Aaron's words rang out together.

"Food that's fit for a king. No one makes better pancakes than your aunt Emily," said his dad.

Cher leaned out of the car and reached for her brother's arm. She pulled him close to her. "I didn't know we had an Aunt Emily."

"We're not really related. She's a friend of the family." That much he knew. "You wouldn't remember her at all. You were a baby the last time we saw her. I was five."

The truth was that Aaron didn't remember much of Aunt Emily either, but his father had assured him that when he was five he had adored her. Her daughter, Millicent, was a different story. The last time they met, she was a gum-cracking teenager who called him Wonder Boy. Even at five, a kid is bound to remember the person who calls him Wonder Boy.

A light snapped on. Two women burst from the door. They stood on the front porch. Then they skirted around the spiderweb and hurried down the side steps.

"Hey, Wonder Boy," said the younger one. "How've you been?" Millicent had the same dark hair and the same

get-down-to-business walk she'd had when she was a teenager, but she was old now. About twenty-three at least.

It was Aunt Emily who reached him first. She threw her
arms around him. "You poor kid." Something about the way
she hugged made him like her right away. Cher must have liked
her too. She slowly released her grip on her brother's arm, got
out of the car, and stood beside him.

His father and Aunt Emily had some quick whispered conversations. Then he handed her Aaron's suitcases and other
bags from the trunk. When his dad tried to give her a wad of
money, Aunt Emily shook her head. "No, no. He won't need
any here."

While the adults talked, Cher pulled him away from the
others. "Do you really want to do this? Are you sure?" she asked.

"I'll be fine," he said. "It's only for a little bit. And I need a
break." But even his seven-year-old sister wasn't fooled by his
fake smile. She threw her arms around him and hugged him
tight.

There were more hugs, except this time they were good-
byes. His father and Cher grabbed him at the same time. As
he stood sandwiched between them, Aaron wasn't sure if he
heard the swishy sound of the wind or if his father had whispered the words "I'm sorry."

As soon as they drove away, Millicent patted him on the
back. "Well, kid, I guess you're incognito now."

Incognito. The word sounded musical and he liked that.

Incognito. It meant driving to New Jersey in the middle of the night.

It meant staying with Aunt Emily, whom he hardly remembered, and Millicent, who still snapped loudly when she chewed her gum.

It meant changing his name to Aaron.

It meant hiding out at the Pancake . . . Palace.

He was still standing outside on the gravel driveway wondering what else *incognito* meant when Millicent ran her hands through his long curly hair. "This," she said, "has got to go."

Snip. Snip.

The inside of the Pancake Palace was nicer than the outside. It was cozy. But not super cozy. And clean. Not glistening or shining or spotless. Just clean. There were nine tables, ten if you counted the two-seater tucked into the corner. The walls were filled with pictures of the pine trees and streams and sand hills. They were nice pictures, but nothing special, the type of thing you'd forget as soon as you left the place.

But then Aunt Emily flicked on a switch. Some lights went on and a radio blared. And the song that shook through the room? That was memorable. Loudly memorable. Guitars screamed. Drums rumbled through the floor. Millicent shouted, "Hey, Mom! Do you have to play that now? We have company." She pointed to Aaron.

"I love this song." Aunt Emily jumped around the tables playing an imaginary guitar. "Here's my favorite part." She stomped her feet in time with crashing cymbals.

"Welcome to my world." Millicent had to shout into Aaron's ear. "You never know what she's going to listen to once the customers leave." She hurried over to the counter and snapped off the radio. Right in the middle of a raging drum solo, the music faded.

"Hey," protested Aunt Emily. "I wasn't finished." She gave her air guitar a few more strums.

Now the only sounds left were the drip-drip of a leaky faucet and a ceiling fan that was slightly out of balance, so instead of whirring along, it went "Whir chink. Whir chink. Whir chink."

And there was the sound of Aaron's shallow breath.

He ran his hands along the polished wood counter and his mouth watered for fries. He'd been in places like this hundreds of times. And they always served curly fries.

"This is the restaurant part." Aunt Emily waved her hand around the room. "Back there is my griddle. You already saw where the radio is." She pointed toward a closet. "That's where we keep our music. We have quite a collection in there, and it's not just heavy metal. Feel free to take a listen anytime you want." Then she pointed at a door. "Back there are the bedrooms, the living room, the den, and another kitchen. It's where we live."

Millicent grabbed his suitcases and headed toward the back of the house. She returned waving scissors. "Ready for your cut?"

Aaron pushed his curls behind his ears. "Can't I just slick it back?"

Millicent snipped the scissors in the air. "Your hair is as famous as you are. If you want to stay, it has to go."

This wasn't the first time he'd faced a scissor-wielding hair-stylist. All his life, people in fancy salons, day spas, and barbershops had run their hands through his long curls, offering to give him a cut. A new look. A little trim. "Never let anyone touch your hair," his father warned. "Not too many guys can grow it long like that and look good in it." His dad was right—it had become his signature style. But all that was before. Now he was incognito. His father had never counted on his being incognito.

Aaron followed Millicent and Aunt Emily to the bathroom and inched his way onto the edge of the tub.

When the first lock of hair fell to the floor, Aunt Emily gasped. Aaron closed his eyes. It took a few more snips before he could gather up the courage to look down. Lying on the black and white tiles, his hair looked longer than he remembered.

And darker.

And shinier.

"Do you sell curly fries?" he asked. Anything to get his mind off his hair.

"We sell pancakes. Reds. Whites. Or Blues," said Aunt Emily. Another lock drifted toward the floor.

There was a moment of silence. Then Aunt Emily continued. "Reds have cranberries. They're grown out in the bogs, not too far from here. The Blues are made from blueberries picked from the banks of the river, if I can get them. Wild berries are sweeter than the ones you buy in the stores. The Whites are plain, of course. Only there's nothing plain about them. I make the best pancakes in the state of New Jersey."

"Anything else?" he asked. There was still a chance for fries.

"Coffee, tea, and lemonade," said Aunt Emily. "The lemonade is made the old-fashioned way with real lemons. I will not have a powdered mix in my restaurant."

"We're going to have crepes on the menu soon," Millicent chimed in. "The fancy ones with powdered sugar. We need something new to drum up business."

"We don't need crepes. We do fine without them." Aunt Emily's voice went from maple syrup sweet to sharp as scissors. "I will not be like those other diners with their everything-but-the-kitchen-sink menus. How can anyone cook all that stuff well? It's better to serve one food and make it memorable."

Millicent grabbed some hair and snipped a little quicker. "We're still in negotiations on that one. You like crepes, don't you, Wonder Boy?"

He was too distracted by the pile of hair on the floor to answer.

"Sweetie," said Aunt Emily. "I'm going to make you a big stack of all three types. Let me go back into the Palace and fire up my griddle."

Millicent took a few more snips and then stepped back. "Done," she announced. "Now we have to change the color." She held up a box of hair dye and pointed to it, smiling like she was on a television commercial. "See? It's the perfect shade of bland." She ripped open the box. "Good thing I bought this color once by accident."

"You are a hairstylist? Right?"

"No, I'm a librarian." When she said the word *librarian*, Millicent stood up straighter. "Just got my degree a few weeks ago. Haven't landed a job yet." She snapped on a pair of plastic gloves. "Hey, can you keep a secret?"

Aaron, the boy with the new name, nodded.

"I'm applying for a job at a library in Hawaii. I already had an interview, and it looks promising. Think about it. Beaches and books. Can it get any better?" She moved her hips in a hula motion and waved her plastic-gloved hands. "I don't want to jinx it by telling lots of people. Only my mom knows. But I'm a short-timer in this town."

"So have you colored a lot of hair then?"

Millicent finished mixing and poured the liquid on top of his head. "Don't worry. You'll be fine. Besides, this isn't about it coming out good. It's about it coming out different." She began to hum.

"Hey, Mom," Millicent called to the other room. "We need a story. Some reason that we suddenly have an eleven-year-old boy here."

"We could say he's my nephew," Aunt Emily shouted back.

"Jeez. She's not good with this kind of stuff. The woman can't lie to save her life," Millicent said to Aaron. Then she shouted, "Everyone knows your side of the family. We'll have to say he's on Dad's side."

There was no answer.

"Bad divorce," Millicent explained. "But you have to be from my father's side. They hardly know him around here, much less his family. My dad's name is Paul. Can you remember that?"

"Paul," he repeated, but he was terrible with names.

"Maybe you should tell people you're visiting while your parents are on a vacation."

"Both parents?" Aaron asked. His mother had died when

Cher was born. For most of his life it had been him, his dad, and his sister.

"Yeah. People don't ask as many questions if you say you have a mother and a father. Anything else makes them nosy." Millicent shook the bottle again and poured the last of the liquid on the spot behind his ears. "The most important thing is for you to help out. You know. Pour the coffee. Clear the tables. Make yourself useful. It's not about the haircut. It's about you blending in."

"That's going to be hard," he confessed. "I'm told I just naturally radiate." It was the word used in that big article in *Celebrity Scoop Magazine*. "A shining star," it called him. "One that will be remembered for ages."

"Yeah, well, there's no radiating allowed at the Pancake Palace." She took a towel and patted the dye off his face. "One more thing, there are only two kids your age who live in this town. RJ and Cecilia. Keep away from them."

"Why?"

"You can't make friends here. Not if you want to stay incognito. Friends and secrets don't mix."

"They don't mix? How do you know?"

"I'm a voracious reader." Millicent pushed his head into the sink and began rinsing off the dye.

Aaron closed his eyes and let the water rush over him. "Why are you doing this?" he asked finally.

"I already told you. If you don't change your color, they'll recognize you."

"No. Not that." A single drop of water trickled down the back of his neck, and it gave him the shivers. "Why are you and Aunt Emily taking me in?"

"My mom, well, she's one of those good-deed doers who likes to send hugs out into the world. She's also a pushover for musicians. So when your dad called, of course she said yes. Me, I'm in it for the adventure." Millicent winked and he wasn't sure if she was kidding or not. "It's not every day you get to share your home with the most famous superstar."

"Musician," Aaron interrupted. "I'm a musician first." He looked away. "At least, I was."

Millicent nodded. "Big-time celebrity. The most famous one in America."

"In the world. They say I'm the most famous in the world," he said sadly.

"Yeah. Must be rough." Millicent gave his hair a final rinse and then handed him a towel. "There, you're done." She stepped back to admire her work. "No one would ever guess that you're the *world*-famous superstar and musician Elvis Ruby."

"Aaron. My name is Aaron. You'd better call me that, even when we're alone, so no one slips up."

Millicent nodded. "Sure, Wonder Boy, whatever you say." With a great flourish, she held a mirror in front of his face.

His long dark curly hair was gone. In its place was hair that was not brown, not blond, not black. Not stylish, but not shaggy either.

Millicent gave a satisfied nod. "You don't look like you at all. You could be anybody." She grabbed his arm. "Come on, let's show my mom."

Aunt Emily was in the kitchen holding a plate of Reds, Whites, and Blues. When she saw his face, she put the pancakes on the table. "Are you okay?"

Aaron turned and ran. Before he knew it, he was outside in the back yard, standing underneath four shabby trees. He looked up at the sky and he began to cry.

Bad haircuts will do that to you.

If You Stand Near the Trees, You'll Hear Things

Cecilia hadn't meant to be hiding behind the garden bench when the door flew open and the boy ran into the back yard. At least that's what she told herself. But the truth was her curiosity grabbed at her the way sugar sand grabbed at those slippers. Ever since that car drove away, she'd been standing outside the Pancake Palace watching the house lights go on and off, trying to get a glimpse of the new visitor.

The only reason she was able to dive for cover was that her feet were beginning to hurt and the one without the slipper was getting cold, so she'd limped over to the bench to rest. It was dumb luck, really. If it had happened a few minutes earlier she would have been caught red-handed in the middle of the yard.

Again, the back door slammed open. Aunt Emily, who wasn't really Cecilia's aunt but almost everyone in Wares Grove called her that, hurried toward the boy.

He was still crying. His sobs alternated between wails and whimpers. During the wails, he stared up at the sky, wearing a "why me" look. But it was the whimpers that got to Cecilia the most. The bravery in them. The trying so hard to suck it all in.

Aunt Emily placed her hand on the boy's shoulder, and it gave Cecilia the feeling that she'd barged into a very personal and private conversation.

She stared down at her bunny slipper and blushed.

When she looked up again, the sobbing had stopped. They were talking instead. She heard soft murmurs. Aunt Emily rubbed the top of the boy's head and the boy even laughed.

But this wasn't the same person who'd gotten out of the shiny sleek car earlier that night. The person in the car (boy or girl, she still wasn't sure) had long dark hair. *This* boy she would have remembered. *This* boy had short hair the color of moonlight.

Aunt Emily was pointing to the four trees now. One by one, she touched each and every one of them. Still hidden by darkness, Cecilia crept closer so she could listen.

The trees had names. Aunt Emily was telling the boy all about them. The Old Man was the knobby pine with branches that hung down like a beard. Next to it stood the Pregnant Lady, named for its trunk that bulged out big and round. Alongside that was the Thief. "Watch that one. It's always grabbing on to something," Aunt Emily explained.

The boy laughed.

There was one tree left. It leaned so far away from the others that it looked like it was trying to run away. "This"— Aunt Emily patted the trunk—"is Wandering Bill." The wind blew. The branches on Bill rattled the way wandering things like to do, blowing first one way, then another, then every which way at once.

There was a shout from the back door. "Hey, out there." When Cecilia heard Millicent's snappy voice, she scrunched down lower. It would be bad enough to get caught by Aunt Emily, but it would be even worse to get caught by Millicent. "These pancakes are getting cold. And we've got some work to do. We need to come up with a story about why you're here. Did you hear me? Mom? Aaron?" When Millicent said his name, she stretched out the *a* and rolled the *n* so it came out long and hard. "Aaaaronnn."

"Aaron," whispered Cecilia. The crying boy with the moonlight hair. The boy who needed "a story." And the long-haired child from the car earlier that night? Maybe it was a girl. And maybe *she* was sitting inside at the kitchen table eating pancakes.

Maybe there were two of them.

A girl who was eating pancakes.

And a boy with moonlight hair.

She'd find out soon enough. In a small town like Wares Grove, people talked.

The Price of Fame

Back inside the Pancake Palace, the world-famous musician Elvis Ruby (but please call him Aaron) sat at the kitchen table eating pancakes.

"Nothing washes away troubles like blueberry syrup," said Aunt Emily. She handed him a full pitcher and a cup of melted butter. He poured it all on his first stack.

It felt good to stand under those trees and cry. It had been a day of keeping quiet, of hiding under covers, of being very still. A few hours ago, he was holed up in his New York City apartment. Reporters blocked the doorway. Paparazzi stood outside his window, armed with cameras and ready to shoot. "The price of fame," his father had said.

"I want them to go away," he replied. "I want out."

The plan to escape was bold and brash. Jake, his body-guard, had thought of every detail. Cher and his father pretended to go to a movie. Aaron hid in a laundry bag while Jake, disguised as an old man, carried him right out the front door. Aaron could hear the reporters' casual conversations. He could smell the hotdogs the paparazzi were eating for lunch. Jake and his bundle got into a cab, and they rendezvoused with Cher and his father at the car rental place.

"There is such a thing as being too famous," Jake had said before his father drove away. "This boy needs a break. Take him someplace where they won't find him."

"Don't worry," said his dad. "I know the perfect hideout."

For a hired guy, Jake was okay.

The blueberry syrup was working. He finished up his pancakes and waited while Aunt Emily made him another stack. He was calmer now. Aaron could finally touch his hair without going into a full-fledged panic. He rubbed his head and yawned.

"You look tired," said Aunt Emily.

Millicent insisted that he take her bedroom. "I'll sleep in the den. We can't have the most famous boy in the universe snoring on the couch," she said.

When he walked into her room, she threw him a stuffed animal. "His name is Fred. He's as old as me, but you can borrow him. See where he's worn? When I was a little girl, I used to chew Fred's ear." But more than Fred's ear was chewed. The toy was so ragged it was hard to tell what kind of animal Fred once was.

Before he could say thank you, Millicent pointed her finger at him. "Don't you dare tell anyone, but on bad days I still cuddle up with him."

Aaron shrugged the stuffed animal away, mumbling something about kids his age, but he slept with him anyway. At least he tried to sleep. He tossed and turned and slipped into bad dreams. When he bolted up, startled from his nightmares, Fred was always there, and Aaron decided that in his pre-chewed state Fred had been a lion.

When morning finally came, Aaron got out of bed and placed Fred on the dresser, leaning him up against a photo of Millicent standing on the beach with a guy who was tall and reedy, with a scar over his eye and a friendly smile.

Millicent's room was still dark. The night before, Aunt Emily had pulled the curtains so tight that not even a dapple of daylight dared to enter. As long as they were closed, he could pretend he was safe.

There was only one way to know for sure.

He stood in front of the window and opened up the curtains an eyeball-sized crack to take a peek. The sun poured in too much and too fast, and it was like looking up at a giant spotlight, too bright to see.

Aaron took a breath.

And he muttered the words:

"Ready.

"Set.

"Go."

He pulled open the curtains fast, the same way you'd pull off a Band-Aid when you don't want it to hurt. He looked outside.

Nothing.

There were no crowds. No reporters. No pop from paparazzi cameras. Even that goofy blond guy from the television show *TMI* who was famous for jumping out of the bushes to shoot pictures of celebrities was nowhere to be seen. And that guy was *always* there. As far as Aaron could tell, he never ate, slept, or used a bathroom. He was relentless.

There were only those crooked trees, a garden bench, and, beyond that, miles of pines.

If they had followed him, they would have been here by now.

He leaned out the window and felt the cool spring air on his face. This simple thing. It had been months since he could open a curtain and not get his picture snapped. And he couldn't even remember the last time he'd leaned out of a window in the morning.

Maybe his father was right. Maybe no one would find him here.

Someone knocked on the door. "Hey, Wonder Boy. Are you awake?" The bedroom door flung open, and Millicent tossed him a T-shirt. "Wear this. It's the official Pancake Palace uniform."

"It's very green," he said, a little surprised. Aaron never wore green. For as long as he could remember, everything he owned was black. His dad called it his signature color. "Let the others dress flashy. They'll remember you more if you keep it simple."

Aaron pulled the shirt over his head, examining its greenness in the mirror. Millicent straightened out a wrinkle. "It looks nice on you."

"Yes," he said sadly. It was true. Even with hair that had been cut by a librarian and an oversized T-shirt that said "Everyone Eats at Piney Pete's," there was no getting around it. He was a good-looking boy. And good-looking boys draw attention.

Millicent grabbed his arm. "Let's go. The place is packed already. Remember, you need to blend in. Don't make eye contact. Don't smile." They hurried through the den and the kitchen, while Millicent rattled off a list of more don'ts. "Don't be rude."

"I'm never rude," he replied. Superstars who are rude get bad press.

"Don't be overly friendly."

"Got it."

"The most important thing is don't worry." They were approaching the Palace door. Millicent slowed down her pace. "If you worry, they'll sense your fear."

"Sense my fear? What kind of people are you feeding?"

"Look. In a day or two, everyone will be used to you. And you'll be like part of the scenery here. Not much happens in this town, so when a kid shows up out of nowhere in the middle of the night, some of our regulars are going to wonder why. And if you let them, they'll grill you like a pancake." Millicent pointed to the next room. "Be careful in there."

Watch Your Gestures

There's a special trick to being incognito. You have to watch your gestures. Changing your hair helps. A new cut and color never hurt anyone. And Millicent was right. You must do your best to blend in. That will help too.

But if you really need to hide (and it wouldn't be right to ask you why, you'd probably have your reasons), you must change everything. The way you walk. The way you hold your fork. The way you move your body when you hear your favorite song.

A simple gesture can give you away.

A shrug. A wink. A flash of a smile.

It can stir a memory.

If you're world-famous, it could make a stranger look you in the eye and say, "Hey, haven't I seen you before?"

And then the jig is up.

Changing your gestures is the hardest thing to do.

That morning in the Pancake Palace before Aaron even served his first short stack of Blues, Aunt Emily whispered, "You're running your hands through your hair. Careful about that. They'll know it's you."

He had short hair now, but he couldn't help it. Old habits are hard to break.

And twice after he handed out some change, Millicent gave him a sharp elbow. "You're radiating. That smile you gave that customer lit up the whole room. Stop making eye contact. And remember to mumble."

"Right," he said, although it went against everything he'd ever known. Aaron had been trained in the proper way to smile, and it involved looking a person straight in the eye so they can see your inner glow. When you're famous, you have a coach for everything.

"Aaron. Aaron," called Millicent. He forgot to look up. The way you answer when someone calls your name is a gesture too.

Millicent introduced Aaron to the man sitting at the counter. "This is Jacob Clayton. We went to high school together. He's the mechanic next door."

"Hey, aren't you in a picture on the dresser in Millicent's room? At the beach?" asked Aaron, before he remembered he was supposed to mumble.

"Is that right?" Jacob's eyebrows went up so high that the scar over his eye practically disappeared.

"I happened to have an empty frame. That is all." Millicent hurried away with menus for a new table.

A song played on the radio. Millicent's heels clicked out the beat. Aaron began to sway. It was a loud song, just like the one that Aunt Emily had danced around to the night before. He closed his eyes. He moved his feet. He looked exactly like he did onstage when he was about to perform.

The customers noticed. The room grew quiet. Even three-year-old Jack Junior, who was facedown on the floor in the middle of a temper tantrum, looked his way.

Aunt Emily waved her spatula in the air, trying to get his attention. Millicent dropped some cups in the sink and they landed with a clang. "Aaron," she hissed as soon as he finally looked up, "get a hold of yourself."

Jacob Clayton was the first to break the silence. He leaned over the counter. "That boy looks familiar. Has he been here before?"

Aunt Emily stood by the grill and stammered. She poured out more pancakes and waited for them to bubble before she turned them over, one by one.

Millicent jumped in. "Oh, no. You've never met. He's a distant cousin, but people always say we have the same eyes." She patted Jacob's hand. And Jacob stared down at the spot on his skin Millicent had touched, forgetting all about Aaron and his familiar looks.

But not all of the customers were taken in by enchanting smiles from Millicent.

"Hey, kid! Kid!" In the back of the room, a bald man with a plaid shirt and a major attitude held up his empty cup. "When you're done taking your little break up there, can we get some more coffee here?" He turned to his friend who was seated beside him and said something loud about "bad service."

Millicent grabbed the coffeepot before Aaron had a chance. "I'll handle these two. They're tourists from up north. They go kayaking every weekend. All they ever want is coffee. You can't make money when people take up table space for hours. Wish I could ask them to leave, but you can't do that in the restaurant business. Bad tippers too."

Aaron glanced over at their table and noticed both of them tapping their feet to the music. "That's because you're playing their song."

He marched over to the closet that Aunt Emily had shown him the night before and gave a low whistle. It was filled with music. CDs. Cassette tapes. A few iPods. Underneath a pile of old albums, a clunky record player said "Property of Paul." Perfect. It was all perfect. There was every type there too, piles of Aunt Emily's favorites, loud rock songs where both the guitars and the singers screamed. But there was so much more.

Aaron went through a pile of CDs, chose his first song, and hit play. A bass drum went *boom boom boom boom*. High-pitched voices sang the same two words over and over again. "Let's boogie!" It was time for disco.

The kayakers looked out the window and shifted in their seats. They weren't tapping their feet anymore.

The next song was a slow tune where a woman sang the words "Honestly love you" over and over again in a quivering voice. Right in the middle of her most serious heartfelt quiver, the bald kayaker glanced at his check.

Now it was time to seal the deal. Aaron thought about playing a twangy country tune but then thought better of it. Instead he found a collection of Broadway show tunes. *The Lion King. A Chorus Line. The Phantom of the Opera.* Aaron knew them all.

He found the show called *South Pacific* and chose the song "I'm Gonna Wash That Man Right Outta My Hair." Lyrics about washing hair. Female voices singing in harmony. A repetitive, cheerful beat. Perfect for chasing out rude, bald forty-year-old kayakers.

Before the song ended, the two men dropped a twenty-dollar bill on the table and didn't wait for change.

When Aaron looked up, Millicent was standing at the closet door. "That was amazing." She clapped and Aaron took a bow.

Millicent pointed to Andrea and Jack Blades. "Can you do it again? Jack Junior's on his fifth temper tantrum and they're never leaving. My mom keeps giving them free pancakes because she thinks"—Millicent made her voice as round and warm as Aunt Emily's—"that little boy is so adorable."

"Tell me about them," he said.

"They're around my age. Big Jack works sometimes with Jacob Clayton as a mechanic at Barnegat Al's. He drives an SUV. Back in high school, Andrea was always the one with the camera. She loved to take pictures." Millicent pointed to a photo of a flower on the wall. "She took that. Now she has a part-time job down at the local WaWa store." Millicent gave Jack Junior a hard look. "Plus, they've got this little devil of a three-year-old."

Aaron studied the pictures and nodded. Parents of difficult children were used to loud, unpleasant noises. He'd have to avoid music with a heavy beat. Besides, very young children were drawn to such music. If Jack Junior started to bop up and down in time to the song, the Blades would never leave. He'd have to be careful. Three-year-olds were prone to spontaneous dance.

He hit play. The first song was a dainty piano piece. No horns. No drums. Just fast and furious notes played at the high end of the keyboard.

The Power of Song

That's how Aaron's career at the Pancake Palace began. By the end of the week, he could tell which customers would overstay their welcome even before they opened up their menus.

Three songs. He could get rid of anyone in three songs.

Dating couples, too busy gazing into each other's eyes to order food.

Loud cell phone talkers.

Low tippers.

It didn't matter who it was. As soon as Millicent gave him the nod, it was time for them to go.

It's not as easy as it seems. You can't disturb the eating, paying customers. You have to target your songs carefully.

If he did it right (and he always did it right), the ones he

The second song was soft and sad. Big Jack stirred his coffee in time to the mournful violins.

In the third song a man with a syrupy voice poured his heart out. The lyrics were sticky and sweet.

It sent them scampering.

Andrea pulled Jack Junior into her arms and headed toward the door. After paying the check, Big Jack grabbed Jack Junior's toys and ran off after her.

"Come back again. Tomorrow we have a Pancake Dinner Special," said Millicent. She was all smiles.

The other customers hardly noticed. Aunt Emily was still turning pancakes at the griddle.

Mission accomplished.

Millicent gave him a high five down low. "How'd you learn to do that?"

"From my dad, I guess."

His father always said that a performer who doesn't know how to read a crowd isn't worth his salt. "You have to play what people want to hear," his father said. "That's how you become memorable."

"I know what kind of music people like." Aaron waved toward the empty tables. "I guess I also know what kind of music gets on their nerves."

Millicent smiled. "Well, Wonder Boy, it seems there is no end to your talents."

chased away never knew why they wanted to leave at the exact moment they did. It was subtle. Their moods would change. Their minds would wander. They'd gather up their things. They'd never think it was the music.

But that is the power of a song.

It can keep you or it can make you want to go away.

And songs had other powers too. Every time he played one, he felt a little more like he belonged. He was a working boy again and it made him feel useful. He had a job: Chief Song Picker at the Pancake Palace. Every time he chased out a customer, he felt a little more like Aaron, the boy he was pretending to be, and a little less like Elvis Ruby, the superstar/musician he was.

There was a certain comfort in that.

The worst time. The hardest time was 8:04 p.m.

8:04 p.m. is the most musical time of the day.

At 8:04 in New York City, curtains go up on Broadway. Most people think the shows start at 8:00. That's what the tickets say. But they give the audience four minutes to wait, to anticipate.

At 8:04 on every musical reality show on television, the best singers perform. It brings in the viewers. Then, if that singer performs later in the show, you've captured your audience for the entire night.

Even shows in little theaters, traveling shows too, start at 8:04. His sister, Cher, was in a traveling show, playing the youngest daughter in *The Sound of Music.* He could imagine Cher waiting to go on, dressed in heavy makeup, filled with confidence that only seven-year-olds have. By eight you start to wonder if you missed a note or if you were at your best. Seven is the year before you turn shy.

Aaron was glad Cher was there performing. And he told himself it didn't matter that he wasn't. But then every night 8:04 would come around, tap him on the shoulder, and remind him of his dream.

At 8:04 he hated being Aaron.

At 8:04 he wanted to play music and sing.

Some nights at 8:04 he'd sneak out behind the Pancake Palace and stand underneath those four trees.

And say his name out loud and tell them about all those 8:04s, where he sang in front of an audience and he shone.

Trying to Get Info from Mrs. Herbert

Cecilia was surprised there was never any mention of the person with long dark hair. That night the shiny car pulled up and Aaron came to town, she was positive she saw a dark-haired person go into the Pancake Palace.

She tried to ask around.

Once she ran into Jacob Clayton as he was hurrying from Barnegat Al's Auto Repair to have dinner at the Pancake Palace and asked him. "Nope. There's only one boy. He has short hair. And I would know. I never miss a meal there." He winked. "Millicent would have told me if there was another."

She walked Storm a dozen times a day past the Pancake Palace looking for the kid with dark hair. And she almost blurted what she saw that night the car came into town to Mrs. Herbert, because if anyone knew what was going on, Mrs. Herbert would. Sometimes you have to give someone information to get some in return.

"It's only one boy? Are you sure?" asked Cecilia again when she met Mrs. Herbert on the front porch of the Lost Treasures Thrift and Throwaway Store. Storm sniffed at the floor.

"Positive." Mrs. Herbert sat down in a wicker rocking chair, then patted the chair next to her, motioning for Cecilia to sit too.

It was Mr. Herbert's favorite chair, and even after all these months since he'd passed away, it didn't feel right to sit in it. Instead of sliding all the way back, Cecilia parked her rear end on the corner, leaving the rest of the seat empty, as if Mr. Herbert were still alive and sitting next to her. "There's no girl?" she asked.

"Oh, sweetie, I know why you keep asking. I bet you were hoping for a girl so you could have a new friend." Mrs. Herbert made that tsk-tsk sound and Cecilia stared down at the floor. Nothing embarrassed her more than when grownups caught her feeling lonely.

"What color is his hair?"

"We've been through this before. It's not really much of a color, I guess. A brown, maybe."

"Are you sure?" asked Cecilia. "It wasn't that blondish brown color that looks like moonlight?"

"Phst." Mrs. Herbert waved her hand, swatting the thought away. "I would have remembered if it was the color of moonlight. It wasn't anything, Cecilia. It was plain old regular hair."

Cecilia leaned back into the chair, thinking. She put her chin in her hand, the way Mr. Herbert used to do when he leaned back, lost in his thoughts.

Mrs. Herbert noticed and let out a long "Hmmmmmm." It wasn't a sigh exactly, although Mrs. Herbert was a sigher. The slightest thing could set her off: coffee that was not brewed fresh, litterers, or when customers at the thrift store pointed to a price tag and asked, "Can't you do any better than that?" But this was different. The deep heavy noise didn't come from Mrs. Herbert's lungs. This sound came straight from her heart.

Cecilia took a breath and made the same "Hmmmmmm" back. She hoped that Mrs. Herbert knew it meant "I understand. I miss him too."

Across the street, RJ ran toward the Pancake Palace. Mrs. Herbert pointed to him. "Since Aaron came to town, he runs back and forth about five times a day. He races into the Pancake Palace but he always leaves alone. I never see the two boys together. I wonder why?"

When RJ saw Cecilia, he waved. This time it was Cecilia's

turn to sigh. A year ago he would've called her over. They would have gone in together.

Mrs. Herbert grabbed Storm's leash. "I'll take care of the puppy for a while if you want to go meet the new boy too."

Cecilia slunk deeper into her seat.

"You haven't met him yet. Have you?" She pushed Cecilia in the direction of the Pancake Palace. "Go."

A Regular Plain-Haired Boy

When RJ saw Cecilia coming across the street, he walked faster.

He was hoping to speak with the new boy alone. He had tried many times before, but every time he walked into the Pancake Palace, the boy seemed to sneak away. He had never met a boy as shy as Aaron. The last thing he needed was Cecilia Wreel at his side.

No one was better than Cecilia when it came to racing down sandy paths or swimming in the streams. She never flinched at water snakes, even the monster one that liked to sun itself down by the pond.

But when they were with other kids, it was different. At school, she'd get so *excited* about things, like the day their teacher showed them how to make electricity from fruit and she jumped up and down and waved her hands shouting "Oh I know. I know" every time Mrs. Montañez asked a question. RJ had to admit it was pretty cool to see a lightbulb lit up by a kumquat, but some control was needed. There were other kids around. And in the cafeteria, where you were supposed to make noise, Cecilia was quiet. RJ watched her that day when Natalie Bracer dropped her hair clip and Cecilia found it. Instead of shouting out "Oh! Oh! Oh! Here it is!" like you'd expect her to, Cecilia picked it up and slipped it in her pocket. And all afternoon when Natalie Bracer hunted through the halls, whining about her messy hair, which was never really messy, Cecilia said nothing.

She was so unpredictable.

The day of the kumquat, he took her aside. "You can't blurt. It's not what the other kids do. And you should give that hair clip back." When he said it, her entire face shrank behind those big glasses. But he did it for her own good. She was too old to be a blurter. And too nice a person to be a hair-clip thief.

She was right behind him. RJ heard her footsteps. He changed his pace to double time. When he got to the door of the Pancake Palace, he and Cecilia were neck and neck. He nodded hello.

The breakfast crowd had thinned out. There were only a few tables full of customers. Millicent was taking care of them.

Aunt Emily sifted flour in the corner. Aaron was pouring maple syrup into little containers.

RJ hurried toward him, but Cecilia stopped in her tracks and hung back by the counter.

Good. It would give him a chance to talk. He was planning on taking a very direct approach. "Hi, Aaron. I have a basketball hoop in my yard if you want to shoot some hoops."

Aaron shrugged.

RJ wasn't sure what kind of answer a shrug meant. "How about soccer? Or skateboards?" he added. "Or ride bicycles, if you don't mind riding my sister Elizabeth's bike. She doesn't use it much anymore."

"Can't," Aaron mumbled.

"Or tennis?" RJ didn't really know why he said tennis. He had never played in his life. If Aaron said yes, he'd manage to find a tennis racket. There was probably an old one lying around in the garage someplace.

"No, thanks."

"Or watch TV?"

Aaron licked the syrup off his fingers and stared down at the ground. "Don't think so."

"Or play video games?" RJ wasn't going to give up that easily. School was a few towns over, and around these parts eleven-year-old boys were in short supply. "Or bake humongous chocolate chip cookies? Or listen to music?"

Suddenly, Millicent was standing by Aaron's side. "Nope. He's not interested," she said.

It was kind of odd, her jumping in like that.

RJ ignored it and asked Aaron another question. "Where are you from anyway?"

"Iowa," said Millicent. Now she was answering for him too. "It's an official Iowa state holiday, which is why he's not in school. He's a cousin on my dad's side. His parents are on vacation." Then she added, "A world cruise. Any more questions?"

RJ shook his head.

Cecilia was standing next to him now. From the way her eyes grew big and her mouth hung open, RJ knew what was going to happen next. She was going to blurt.

"I love your hair," she gushed. "It's better than any other kind." She put her hand over her mouth right after that. She knew what she had done.

Aaron took a few gigantic steps back. Who could blame him?

RJ shrugged. No wonder Natalie Bracer and the other girls at school kept their distance from Cecilia. What a weird thing to say.

Millicent grabbed Cecilia with two hands and bent down to her level and looked her straight in the eye. "It's nothing special. His hair is very plain. He's a typical short-haired boy."

RJ pulled Cecilia by the arm. "Come on, C, let's get out of here."

Be Careful When You Talk to the Trees

That afternoon, when Cecilia got home from the Pancake Palace, the kitchen smelled like brownies. Her mother put two on a plate and set them on the table. They were still warm.

"Your birthday dinner is coming up so soon," she said. "I thought we could talk."

This was not a conversation Cecilia wanted to have. She thought about heading to her bedroom to avoid it, but the brownies were moist and rich and fudgy. A stronger person could perhaps push them away, but when Cecilia saw they were filled with little morsels of chocolate chips, she was too weak to resist. She sat down at the table and chewed, while her mom poured two glasses of milk.

"Did you want to invite some girls from school?" her mom asked.

Cecilia shook her head. There were no girls from school. Not anyone who would come. She thought about asking the Craw twins, Tiffany and Taffy. They let her sit at their table during lunch, but it's not like they ate together. Cecilia sat on one end while the twins traded sandwiches and gossip on the other.

"RJ," she said, hoping that he would be enough. "And Uncle Frank?"

Her mom nodded. "Of course, Uncle Frank."

Storm begged for treats by doing a trick. Cecilia and Mom laughed, because even in the middle of awkward conversations, there is something very funny about watching a long chubby dog run around in circles chasing after his tail.

Her mom grew serious. "Your father and I had a long discussion. Your dad will tell your story about the song and the pines, like he always does. He promised."

It was the first mention of it since that night her mother revealed her theory of too much happiness and endorphins and brain clouds. And Cecilia didn't know quite what to say. She kicked her chair with her feet. "Only Dad will tell the story?"

Her mother nodded. "It will be a nice day." Instead of looking up, she played with some crumbs on her plate. "And I'll make ham and all your favorite foods, like always."

But it wasn't like always. Like always meant her mother would be telling the story too.

Cecilia spent the next few nights climbing out her bedroom window and onto the sugar-sand path. She walked instead of running. She tiptoed by the goldfish pond and the old shed. But always when she got to the spot where the yard ended and the pines grew thick and dense, she stopped.

Cecilia had grown up in the pines. She knew about the night creatures. Wolves. Coyotes. And shadows.

Every night Cecilia walked up and down behind the houses of Wares Grove, right along the brink of the woods, wanting to go in.

And not wanting to.

And wanting to.

And kicking the sand with her slippers.

She had new ones now. They were green corduroy and very sensible. Her mother bought them when she noticed her bunny slipper was missing. She never asked Cecilia about it and of course Cecilia never volunteered.

But on the night of the full moon, the light reached through the trees, and that made Cecilia feel brave. She set out on the sugar-sand path that twisted and turned. She kept watch on the lights of Wares Grove, careful not to go too deep. Somehow, she meandered over near the back yard of the Pancake Palace.

There underneath those four trees was Aaron.

The moonlight shone on his hair.

She moved closer.

He was talking to the trees.

This was worse than overhearing a conversation between him and Aunt Emily.

The boy was *talking* to the *trees*.

He said his name out loud.

He said his real name.

And she knew who he was.

She turned and ran, not caring if she made noise or caused a tree limb to stir or lost a slipper in the sugar sand. She bolted toward the house and clamored up the window, forgetting about the fact that sleeping parents woke up easily.

When she got inside, she ignored Storm's licks and jumps and turns, which was something she never did. She dived underneath the bed and pulled out a box. There was Natalie Bracer's pink scrapbook. On the cover surrounded by purple crayon hearts and lots of X's and O's was the boy's name.

Elvis Ruby.

Superstar. Celebrity. Musician.

The most famous boy in the world.

Hiding out at the Pancake Palace.

A Devilish Pinelands Tale

Here's a little secret about the Pinelands of New Jersey. Over the years, it's been filled with hiders. Misfits. Thieves. Pirates. Smugglers. And good, decent people looking for peace and quiet. They've all sought refuge in the Pinelands' sandy soil.

The most famous hider (before Elvis Ruby, of course) was the thirteenth child of a certain Mrs. Leeds. He was a different sort of boy, a crooked twig from the family tree. They say that not long after he came into the world, he sprouted bat wings, horns, and a serpent's tail, then flew away to hide among the sand hills and salt marshes. His real name was long forgotten. They call him the Jersey Devil. They say he's out there still.

Sounds crazy, right?

But to this day, if you ask around, you'll find people who say they've seen him. You can't go into a Pinelands restaurant or gift shop without finding his image plastered all over the place. In Wares Grove he's everywhere. At the Lost Treasures Thrift and Throwaway Store there's an entire shelf dedicated especially to him. A Jersey Devil jelly jar. A floaty pen with the Jersey Devil inside the cap. And there are those really awful souvenir salt and pepper shakers.

At the Pancake Palace, he's on their official T-shirt, sitting in front of a plate of steaming Reds, Whites, and Blues just above the words "Everyone Eats at Piney Pete's." He's also on their place mats. It was all Millicent's idea.

Elvis Ruby wore that T-shirt too. It's kind of funny. A hider wearing a picture of another hider. But Elvis never looked at it that way. Sometimes hiders are too busy hiding to see the humor.

But then again, when you're a hider things can get very serious very fast.

Cecilia Waits

It was closing time on the following night. Most of the customers were on their way out when Cecilia marched into the Pancake Palace and sat at the two-seater in the back.

She buried her face in a menu, studying it like it was complicated, even though secretly she wondered why they even bothered with a menu since all they had were three types of pancakes and most people knew exactly which ones they were going to order anyway.

"Can I help you?"

When Cecilia looked up, Millicent was standing by the table, looming over her like an old willow.

"I'm still deciding," mumbled Cecilia.

"There's not much time," Millicent snapped. She pointed to the clock.

The only other customer left in the Palace was Jacob Clayton, who sat at the counter absentmindedly rubbing his hand over his good luck scar. "It's not the nicest-looking scar in the world but it has to be good luck," he told Cecilia that time when she forgot it was impolite to stare. "If that fish hook was a little lower, it would have caught my eye, so it's a good thing it landed where it did." Cecilia noticed that Jacob wasn't eating anything either, and you could bet that Millicent wasn't going to be talking to *him* in that snappy way.

Aaron and Aunt Emily were in the back kitchen. Cecilia could see their shadows moving about through the half-opened door.

Aaron.

"So have you decided yet?" asked Millicent, still looming.

Cecilia glanced back over the menu. In two words, she could turn Millicent from a giant tree of a person into a wilted little seedling. She could imagine Millicent shrinking away. She could picture the look on her face if she blurted it out.

"I know," Cecilia wanted to say. "I know who he really is."

And she almost did it too. When someone is looming over you, looking at you like that, there comes a point.

But then Aunt Emily appeared at the table and handed her a bag of pancakes. "Cecilia, sweetie, take these home with you.

They're still hot. I put some extra Reds in there because I know they're your mom's favorites."

So instead of blurting, Cecilia left with the pancakes in her hand. She sat outside on the bench, nibbling on the Reds and keeping a sharp watch on the Pancake Palace.

A few minutes later, Millicent and Jacob walked out arm in arm. They got into Millicent's car and drove away.

The kitchen light went on. Cecilia could see Aunt Emily's silhouette by the sink arranging wildflowers in mason jars.

With Millicent gone and Aunt Emily busy, he would be alone now.

Elvis Ruby would be by himself.

Cecilia moved so fast up the side steps of the Pancake Palace that the spiderweb that stretched along the porch shook. The patterns of moonlight on the wooden floor jiggled.

The door was open. The room was empty. Cecilia slid into a nearby booth, opened up the pink scrapbook, and began to read. She would wait.

Doc Bashful

Aaron was so busy trying to juggle the arrangements of wildflowers Aunt Emily had given him that he didn't see Cecilia right away. It's a good thing she had her head down in that pink book.

He knew her from Millicent's warnings. He remembered her from the day she came in with RJ.

What was she doing here anyway?

It didn't matter. He could make her go away. A few carefully picked out tunes and she'd be history.

Aaron slid the flowers on the table and crept toward the closet. It was another one of his many talents. He knew how to tiptoe. Years of dance class with Madam Marguerite in that stuffy New York City studio made him light on his feet. He reached the closet and Cecilia never looked up.

He turned off the radio and hit play. He started with a Frank Sinatra tune. Aaron loved this song. Frank's voice is jazzy. The horns sing along. The drums invite the band to swing. But most kids his age didn't share his love. By the time the trombones got wild and loud, she would be ready to leave.

But Cecilia didn't budge. Whatever she was reading had her full attention.

So much for mid-tempo dance music.

He reached for another oldie where the refrain was "doo-wop doo-wop doo-wop." And he looked over at the table, watching her every move.

She was so regular. Average height. Plainly dressed. Except for those out-of-fashion glasses, nothing about her stood out. His father had a special name for people like her. He called them "Doc Bashfuls."

"Ask someone to name the seven dwarfs," he'd say, "and they always forget either Doc or Bashful. You know why? They don't have charisma." His father waved his hands in front of him whenever he said the word. "Charisma is the ability to shine. Grumpy. Happy. Dopey. Everyone remembers them. Those are ones that are filled with star power." Then his father would ruffle his hair and say, "Just like you."

The doo-wop music was over, and Cecilia Wreel sat with her face in that book and her elbows on the table.

Aaron tried a French horn solo.

Cecilia tapped her foot. That was the last thing he expected. An eleven-year-old with a French horn obsession. But her tapping was not in time with the beat. It was oddly placed, first fast, then slow, then slow fast slow fast.

He played a polka.

Same irregular taps.

Then a folk song from Romania.

She shuffled her feet, she kicked under her seat, but it had nothing to do with music.

He reached for a funeral march. Funeral marches were only used in extreme circumstances. And only when there were no other customers around. He hit play and waited.

No sad, sorrowful look. No wistful gaze. Funeral marches always cause sad, sorrowful looks and wistful gazes.

He was desperate and searching now, leaning over those old albums that said "Property of Paul," trying to find a song that would make her leave when he heard her shout. "Hey, Aaron!"

He turned up the volume. The funeral march grew louder. More solemn.

"Hey, Aaron," she called again. "Did you hear me?"

It was getting awkward. He'd have to turn around soon. He had only one more chance to find a song.

She was standing right behind him now. He could see her shadow in the door.

"Hey, Elvis Ruby," she shouted. "What are you doing there?"

That's when he turned off the music.

TweenStar

The sound of his own name startled him. He hadn't heard anyone say it out loud since the night he came to New Jersey.

"How did you find out?" he asked, stunned.

"It's all here." She waved what she'd been reading in front of him. It was a pink scrapbook with swirly stars plastered all over it. He knew what it was. He'd seen hundreds of them. They were handmade collections of articles from newspapers and magazines mixed in with ticket stubs and concert programs, filled with stickers of hearts and stars. Funny, he wouldn't have taken Cecilia Wreel for the scrapbook type. Usually the girls who created scrapbooks wore sparkly earrings, chewed a lot of gum, and wore way too much of the color purple.

Cecilia skipped over to a nearby table, flopped down in a seat, and began flipping through the pages.

He recognized the articles. *New York Post. Celebrity Scoop Magazine. Los Angeles Times.* He knew them all.

"Your whole life in this book," she said. "Pages and pages of it. Look. Here's what it says about you." She read aloud. "Elvis Ruby: musical prodigy and top-rated contestant on *TweenStar.* Father: Austin Ruby, guitar player for famous rock stars. Sister: Cher, seven-year-old singer. Mother: deceased." Cecilia tried to reach over and pat him on the arm, but he was too far away. "I'm sorry," she said.

He stared down, too surprised to answer.

There was a long, uncomfortable silence before Cecilia continued. "Your favorite song is 'Heartbreak Hotel.' Favorite book: *Bud Not Buddy* by Christopher Paul Curtis. Favorite food: peppermint ice cream and curly fries, but not mixed together." She looked up. "Ha. That's clever."

It was. The *TweenStar* publicity people had told him to say it like that. They coached him about everything.

He could run, but where would he go? His father was on the road touring with Cher. They moved around so much that Elvis couldn't even remember which city they were in. It would be hours before they could get here.

It was better to wait, find out what Cecilia wanted. Who

knows? Maybe she could be bought off with an "Elvis Ruby" autograph.

"Oh, look," said Cecilia. "It says here that you're left-handed." She smiled. "Me too. My mom read an article once where it said that left-handed people are more creative."

Awesome, he thought, waiting for her to get to the point.

She twirled her hair and looked up at the ceiling, like she was going to say something more, but then turned back to the articles. "Here's a headline I don't understand. 'Elvis Ruby, Long Live the King.'"

"I was named for Elvis Aaron Presley. They called him 'the king of rock and roll.'"

"Oh, so that's why you use the name 'Aaron.'" She smiled. "That's clever too.

"You hate yoyos and brussels sprouts." She chewed her lower lip. "Really? Brussels sprouts? My mom makes them. They're loaded with vitamins and they're very tasty if you cook them right."

Elvis looked down at the scratches on the floor.

Ever since that night his father dropped him off here, he had thought about what it would be like if someone discovered his true identity. He often imagined all the different ways it could happen. A teenage girl grabbing on to him and screaming his name. An old man spitting out his blueberry pancakes when he finally discovered the person who had been pouring his coffee was Elvis Ruby. A small wide-eyed toddler tugging at his shirt, saying, "Aren't you? Aren't you . . . ?" There would be shouting and cheers and cameras. And he imagined all the different things they would say and what he would say back. But no matter how many times he thought about this moment, and no matter how many different ways he imagined it, it never involved a Doc Bashful of a girl, a pink scrapbook, and conversations about brussels sprouts.

Cecilia had turned the page again. "Oh, and look at this." She grew so excited, she jumped up and down in her seat until her glasses slid off her face and onto the floor. "They say you're 'legendary.' Imagine that. 'A one in a million performer.'" She crawled under the table and her words grew muffled. "I never met anyone who was legendary before."

When she popped up, her glasses were on her face and she went right back to that article. "It says you're a 'ruby that sparkles.'" She looked up. "Ha! Your last name is Ruby."

"It's overused," said Elvis, and he decided if she jumped up and down like that again he was going to make a run for it.

Cecilia's voice grew low. "Here's where it gets really interesting. It says when you were a contestant in that talent show, *TweenStar*, everyone expected you to win. But you didn't."

"Yeah. Thanks for the update."

"It says that one night when you walked out onstage, you choked. The audience waited. And all you did was stand there.

You froze. And in the history of the show *TweenStar*, that's never happened. It says they waited for you to sing, but nothing came out. And everyone in the *TweenStar* auditorium and the entire television audience watched."

Cecilia closed the book. "It must have been awful. Millions of people from every part of the world watching you."

Elvis gave a heavy nod.

"Did they laugh? It would be awful if they laughed."

She leaned over the table, waiting for an answer.

"I don't know," he said finally.

"How could you not know if they laughed?"

Her eyes were huge, magnified by those thick lenses. Elvis couldn't help staring. "I'd rather not talk about it."

"If you don't want to talk about it, that means they laughed," said Cecilia.

Cecilia blinked and Elvis was still staring. He watched her eyes open again before he finally spoke. "It was even worse than it looked on television."

Cecilia played with the point of a gold star that was curling up on the cover of the scrapbook. "It sounds terrible."

"Hey. Wait a minute. You didn't watch? How could you not have watched? It was the most viewed event in the history of television. It was in the news. The gossip magazines. YouTube." He waved his arms. "The world. The world has watched."

"No. Sorry. It's not my type of show."

She had to be lying. All his fans had seen it. Elvis had never met a girl his age who was not a fan. Elvis stared down at the scrapbook. When it came to fans, scrapbook makers were in a class of their own.

Cecilia followed his gaze. "Oh, this isn't mine. I mean it's mine now, but I didn't make it. I found it at school."

"So you never saw what happened?"

She shook her head. "So that's why you were crying that night you first came here," Cecilia said. "I knew it had to be something terrible."

"You saw that too? Under the trees?" This girl was dangerous. She knew everything. "Please," he begged. "I want to stay. It's nice here." He hadn't even decided which type of Aunt Emily's pancakes he liked best. "You have no idea what it's like out there. I need a break."

"That's what your father says." Cecilia reached into a bag and pulled out a copy of *Celebrity Scoop Magazine*. "On page three. 'Elvis is getting the rest he needs, but he'll be back better than ever very soon.'"

"My dad? He's giving interviews?"

Cecilia nodded. "In every issue. My mom subscribes. See. It's a regular weekly column now featuring Austin Ruby. They call it 'Where's Elvis?' They interview your dad first and then they report Elvis sightings."

"Elvis sightings?"

"Yep. There's a nationwide search. And the magazine is offering a reward. People are saying they spotted you everywhere."

He glanced at the clock. It was 8:04. The most musical minute of the day. Even now in the midst of all this, Elvis noticed the time.

"How much?" he asked, but only after the clock said 8:05.

"Huh?"

"How much is the reward?"

"Ten thousand dollars. Can you believe it?"

Frankly, he expected more.

"You've been seen everywhere," said Cecilia. "It says that two second graders and their mom saw you by a school in Pahrump, Nevada. ' "He was very sweet," said eight-year-old Colleen Goode. "He even helped us cross the street." Her friend Leena Singh agreed. "He made sure there were no cars coming and then he told us to go." '

"And you were spotted seven times in DisneyWorld, usually around the Tower of Terror. And on a playground in Austin, Texas. And right outside the penguin house at the Central Park Zoo. It says you were a pinch hitter in a Little League game in Tallahassee, Florida. You hit a home run. And you were sighted by a dozen different people in 7-Elevens throughout the state of Mississippi."

She folded her arms in front of her. "But you're not in any of those places. You're here."

"Is it the money you want?" he asked. "Do you want the reward?"

Cecilia shook her head. "Oh, no. You're a guest here at the Pancake Palace. That wouldn't be—"

"Then what?" he interrupted.

"Hey, Aaron," Aunt Emily called from the kitchen. "Enough work for tonight. Let's watch some TV." She poked her head out. "Hi, Cecilia. I didn't know you were here."

Cecilia scooped up the scrapbook and hugged it tight. "I just came to invite Aaron to dinner next Sunday. Uncle Frank is coming in."

"Really? From Philadelphia?"

Cecilia nodded.

"You should go. It would do you good," said Aunt Emily. "You've done nothing but work since you got here."

Elvis looked up, surprised, then down at the floor. "I don't know."

"You'll like Uncle Frank," said Aunt Emily. "Everybody likes Uncle Frank."

"So you'll come?" asked Cecilia. "It's for my birthday."

"I don't know," he said again. "Maybe."

"I should be heading home." Cecilia hurried out the door. Elvis followed.

She was standing down by the woods.

"You never answered. What did you want?" When you're famous everyone wants something. Cecilia had to want *something*.

Elvis hurried down the stairs and ran right through that giant spiderweb. "Wait! Please." Cobwebs stretched all over him. "Why did you come here? You never said what you wanted."

He raced over to her and stood there out of breath.

"I want," she said in a small voice, "your help."

Not All Tall Orders Are Pancakes

What she wanted? It was a tall order. Cecilia knew it too. What she wanted was to be able to tell him a story . . . a kind of unbelievable story . . . and she wanted him to believe.

Her own mother no longer believed.

How could she ask a stranger, especially a famous one, to do it?

They stood there, facing each other. Elvis brushed the cobwebs from his face.

It had been a long time since Cecilia told anyone new. Wares Grove was such a small town that everyone knew her story. Most of the people who lived here shrugged it off, and whether or not they believed it was true, they accepted it as just another Pinelands tale. In the Pinelands of New Jersey there are more stories than there are needles on trees.

But Elvis Ruby wasn't from around here. He wasn't even from New Jersey.

Cecilia started slow, but soon it all poured out of her.

She told about her parents' camping trip and how she surprised them and came early.

He interrupted her. "Don't they have hospitals here?"

"Of course we do. This is New Jersey."

She told him about the music and how her parents said it was the most beautiful thing they'd ever heard.

He was quiet then.

She showed him the article that her mom saved from *Celebrity Scoop Magazine* about happiness and brain clouds. And told about how it changed her mother's mind.

They both agreed that *Celebrity Scoop Magazine* is a piece of trash.

She told him that her grandfather once heard the song too, when he was a boy picking blueberries. She paused, then stuttered, then repeated herself over and over again in a rambling way.

When she was done, Elvis snickered.

Yes. That's exactly what it was, thought Cecilia. A snicker. For a mega-celebrity superstar, it was not very attractive.

"So the trees sang?" Elvis snickered again.

"I don't know *exactly* if the trees sang. But it came from somewhere. It rang out. It probably went through the trees."

"And you want me to believe this?"

She nodded.

"What makes you think it's true?" he asked.

"Because I know." She pointed to her heart. "Inside me. I know."

Elvis wiped his tongue with his hand, trying to get rid of the cobweb threads. "This is the strangest thing I've ever heard." And coming from Elvis Ruby, that was saying a lot. He had grown up traveling with musicians, and musicians are filled with odd beliefs and superstitions. He met a drummer once who swore he'd be out of beat if he didn't spin his drumsticks three times clockwise before every song. There was Crazy Joe Stand, the best horn player in the business, who refused to blow a note without a silver dollar in his back pocket. And the first time he met a certain very famous blond singer, she took him aside and told him that every note she sang came straight from the angels.

Angels? Maybe. But trees? Singing trees?

"This is crazy," Elvis said. Still, he leaned into the woods to listen.

Cecilia nodded. "Crazy things are often true."

A screech owl trilled. Elvis jumped. "If there really was a song and it played especially for you, wouldn't you remember? Something about it?"

Cecilia gave him a sad smile. "No one remembers their baby days. I have tried. It's all lost."

Elvis never thought about the first time he heard music, but he could sing and he could play instruments before he could talk, and his father told him he tapped his fingers in time to a song when he was three hours old.

"There's a story about a musician, a man who lived a long time ago. A fiddler. They say he heard it. You do play the fiddle, right?" asked Cecilia. "Are you any good?"

Of course he was good. At the end of every episode of *TweenStar* it was his job to play the official *TweenStar* Goodbye Song. He was famous for it. *Celebrity Scoop Magazine* wrote, "Not since the legendary emperor Nero fiddled while the city of Rome burned around him has there been a more memorable performance on the violin than Elvis Ruby's playing the Goodbye Song to the voted-off *TweenStar* contestants."

When he played, there was not a dry eye in the entire *TweenStar* music hall. He had never met a girl her age who didn't know the *TweenStar* theme song.

"The violin," Elvis said. "It's called a violin."

"Isn't that the same thing?"

It was. But his father always told him to say "violin." It sounded more *special*.

"I thought that maybe we could go into the pines and you could play your *violin*. Maybe that would coax it out of the trees. Then we could both hear it. Please," she begged.

"Coax it out of trees? Are you kidding me? That's crazy."

Cecilia stared out into the woods. It was quite dark, really, so she couldn't see more than ten feet in front of her. And it made Elvis wonder what she was watching. "But if it's not crazy, and if it was *your* song that was out there in the woods, wouldn't *you* want to hear it again?" she asked. "Wouldn't you want to hear the very first sound you heard the moment you were born?"

The first sound he heard was probably his mother. She had died so long ago, he couldn't even remember her voice. "Yes. I would," he said.

Cecilia turned and left, kicking up sand behind her.

The Promise

Cecilia hurried down the road. That went okay, she thought, but her heart thumped loud against her chest. It didn't go exactly the way she had imagined. He didn't exactly jump up and down at the idea. And he snickered. She would never have expected a superstar to snicker.

But he listened to her story, and at least it was a start.

He was her first celebrity. Before this the only famous person she'd ever met was Miss Liberty, who also held the title of Miss Football and Miss Big Blue. But that was only at a parade where Miss Liberty, dressed in a turquoise gown and a sparkly tiara, drove in a car plastered with stickers. And then all Cecilia had done was wave. Still, Miss Liberty was nice. She waved back.

Except for when he snickered, Elvis Ruby was nice too.

The thumps inside her weren't going away, so she walked a little faster. When she got to the last house in town, Cecilia turned around and headed back. There was something about knowing every bump and wrinkle in Wares Grove that made it comforting to walk along the road. It helped her think.

She hugged the scrapbook tight.

The girls at school would curl up into little green balls of envy if they knew that she had invited Elvis Ruby to her house and that he had said, "Maybe." They might even be nicer to her, although she doubted that Natalie Bracer would be nice to her for any reason, and she'd be the last person that Cecilia would ever tell.

It was Natalie's scrapbook she held in her hands. All of the girls in that group had pink books with stars on them and they all collected articles on Elvis Ruby. Natalie had professed her love louder than the others, and her friends never challenged her when she announced, "Someday Elvis Ruby and I will get married." Cecilia thought it was a perfectly silly thing for an eleven-year-old to say.

"And we will live in the *TweenStar* mansion forever." Even Cecilia knew that the winner of the *TweenStar* competition only gets to stay in the mansion until next season.

"And we will have two children, twins. A boy and a girl. Isabella and Aiden."

But one day Natalie had announced, "I'm not in love with him anymore!" She tossed her pink Elvis Ruby scrapbook in the garbage can in Mrs. Montañez's classroom. So it wasn't really stealing when Cecilia crept back into the classroom before Mr. Frieze the janitor came to empty out the garbage. He would have thrown it into the giant dumpster and it would have been gone for good.

A week later Natalie joined her friends in a five-girl hug and wailed, "Elvis. Oh, Elvis, I miss you so." Cecilia thought about returning the scrapbook. But when Natalie brushed past her in the hall and said "Move it" under her breath, she decided against it. There are certain things that you can never get back once you toss them away.

Cecilia didn't take the scrapbook because of Elvis Ruby. She only knew about Elvis Ruby because, well, how could anyone not know about Elvis Ruby? It was like not knowing the name of the president of the United States.

She took the scrapbook because she was looking for clues about Natalie. Maybe if she learned a little more about Natalie's group, she could be a little bit more like them. She wouldn't stand out in that terrible way. She could blend in.

And she did learn from the scrapbook. For example, she had never noticed before but Natalie made the dots on her *i*'s into tiny smiley faces. Occasionally, instead of smiley faces, she made them into flowers. And the whole scrapbook smelled of raspberry bubblegum. It was the special scent of Natalie and her friends. Cecilia began to wonder if it wasn't from the gum at all. Maybe it was a raspberry bubblegum perfume. She would have to look for it the next time she went to the thrift store.

"Hey, Ceily. You've been walking up and down that road forever. What are you up to?"

Cecilia didn't notice RJ until he was almost at her side.

"Just walking," she said.

"No. I've been watching you from my front porch. I can tell by the way you're pacing back and forth that something's going on."

"Shhhh. No talking here." They were walking past the Old Church. They always stopped talking when they walked by the church. Always.

It seemed that RJ forgot.

"Jeez. We were little kids when we first did that. I don't even remember how it started." RJ shoved his hands into his pockets, rolled his eyes up at the sky, but he didn't say another word until they stepped in front of the Wares Grove Hunt Club and she motioned that he could speak again. "Are you going to tell me what's going on?"

She wanted to, but the problem with RJ was that he was

chatty. And Cecilia knew from experience that chatty people sometimes slipped. She moved the scrapbook to her other hand and walked holding it behind her back. Fortunately, RJ wasn't the type to notice books.

"So are you coming to my house for dinner on Sunday? Uncle Frank is coming." Cecilia changed the subject. There were no streetlights in Wares Grove. But Mrs. Herbert's house and her store were both lit up bright. Ever since Mr. Herbert died, she left the lights on even when she slept.

"Sure I'll come. I come every birthday. I like your uncle Frank."

"Everybody likes Uncle Frank."

"Anyone else coming? I mean from school?"

Cecilia caught the worry in his voice.

"No," she said, and RJ's steps looked quicker and lighter. It made her sigh. "But I did invite the boy from the Pancake Palace."

"Aaron?" RJ made a sour face. "And he said yes?"

Cecilia nodded.

"I don't like that kid. He's a shrugger. When you talk to him, all he does is shrug."

"There's a reason for that," said Cecilia, feeling like a fizzy bottle of Coca-Cola that was all shaken up and about to explode. "A really good reason."

"What's his story?" asked RJ.

Cecilia shook her head. "I shouldn't say."

When they reached the other end of town, at the exact same time in the exact same spot they turned around.

They always turned like that, ever since they were little kids and were allowed to go out on their own. The memories of those first walks with RJ softened her. Before she knew it, she was blurting, "He's not who he says he is. He's not who you think. He's hiding out. People are looking for him."

RJ snapped his fist into the palm of his hand. "Ha! I knew it! The kid is shady. He never looks you in the eye. What kind of person never looks you in the eye? What'd he do? Punch a teacher? Shake down some preschoolers for lunch money?"

Cecilia giggled. "No."

RJ pointed at his eye and then at Cecilia's and back at his. "Then why can't he look?"

"I can't tell you." She had said too much already.

"You know I'm gonna find out." He studied her and for the first time saw the pink scrapbook in her hands. "What's that?" He reached for it.

She twirled about and tried to spin away. The scrapbook fell out of her hands and landed faceup on the ground.

The glittery stars. The name "Elvis Ruby." The crayoned hearts. They all sparkled under the glow of Mrs. Herbert's living room light.

RJ picked it up and handed it back to her.

"Cecilia Wreel, what are you up to?"

"If I tell you, you'll have to promise not to tell anyone."

RJ nodded.

And when Cecilia told him about Elvis Ruby, RJ was Old Church quiet.

"Promise me ten thousand times that you won't tell anyone," she said.

"I promise not to tell another soul," he said solemnly.

But he only promised once.

Meanwhile Back at the Palace

Elvis Ruby sat on the porch of Piney Pete's Pancake Palace and took hard deep breaths.

Okay, so she knew.

He was found out.

His cover was blown.

Deep breaths.

At least she didn't ask a hundred questions. At least she didn't jump up and down and scream his name. There was nothing more startling than being two feet away from a person and having her shout at you. It happened all the time. They were warned all about it at *TweenStar*. "Fan frenzy," the show's producers said, "is the most dangerous thing you will ever encounter."

"The price of stardom," his father said.

At least she didn't try to rip off his shirt like those girls in front of the *TweenStar* music hall. They slipped past the body-guards, surprising him and the other contestants when they were doing an interview on national television. Most of the others got away, but they cornered him and Ramon.

They grabbed at his shirt. The fabric, some sort of a miracle blend of cotton and polyester, never ripped. Instead, it twisted around his neck. He choked and gasped for air until a *TweenStar* security guard pulled the girls away.

Ramon was his toughest competition and his closest friend. He could play a bass guitar better than anyone (maybe even better than Elvis's father). He knew how to handle the fans too. He slid off his shirt when the fans circled him. And the girls screamed. Ramon stood there, shirtless, flexing his muscles. "Dude, it was the only way. They would have choked me."

The cameras flashed. The paparazzi loved it. "*TweenStar* Contestant and Bass Guitar Player Ramon Hevia Shows Off Muscles to Adoring Fans," said the headlines the next day.

Ramon could always make him laugh. Even now he'd bet Ramon could find something to make him smile. Elvis thought back to the events of the day, trying to find some morsel of humor. But there was nothing funny about being covered with cobwebs in the middle of New Jersey.

Maybe it wouldn't be over.

Maybe he could still be incognito.

Cecilia Wreel was only one person. As long as he went along with her and looked for that song, he didn't think she'd tell. What harm would it do if one more person knew?

One More Thing

"What are you both thinking? Are you crazy?" Millicent said later that night when she heard that Elvis was going to dinner. "Someone is going to find out."

Aunt Emily added some sugar to the blueberries and stirred them in a pot. "There's not going to be a lot of people there. Cecilia, her parents, her uncle Frank of course, and probably RJ. It will be good for him. He needs to be around people his own age." She took a spoonful of the syrup and gave it to Elvis.

It tasted a little bit sweet, a little bit tart, and almost as good as peppermint ice cream.

"Look at him." Millicent grabbed his arm and waved it in front of Aunt Emily, almost like she forgot that the rest of him was attached to it. "Our boy Aaron here has a remarkable resemblance to the superstar Elvis Ruby. Stick a wig on him with long dark curly hair, and they'll spot him in a minute."

Aunt Emily put her hands on his shoulders and said in a tone filled with great seriousness, "Elvis, I forbid you to put on any long curly wigs at Cecilia's house."

"It's not funny, Mom." Millicent picked up a pile of mail on the kitchen counter and flipped through the envelopes. When she was done, she tossed them on the table without opening a single one. "Is this all the mail there is?" she asked.

Aunt Emily nodded. "Do you really think it's best for him to stay here with us and mope?"

Millicent reached for the mail again and tossed it back on the table. "You'd mope too if you were singing in front of millions one minute and slinging pancakes in this tiny town the next minute. What a letdown. The kid was a huge star and now look at what he's doing."

Elvis hadn't thought it was possible for every word in a sentence to feel like a slap across his face. But each word had its own particular sting.

Aunt Emily walked away from the pot. Then she turned around. "He's not slinging pancakes. *I'm the one* who makes the pancakes. And I don't *sling* them." It seemed Millicent's words slapped her too, although for an entirely different reason.

"*He's* in the room listening to both of you." Elvis pointed to himself. Then he grabbed the spoon and stirred the pot. The berries hissed.

"Don't make him go," said Millicent.

"I'm not making him go," said Aunt Emily.

"I want to go," said Elvis. And even he was surprised at his announcement. I need to go, he thought.

There were ten thousand reasons for him to go.

"People see him all the time here," said Aunt Emily. "We haven't exactly kept him locked up in the cupboard under the stairs."

"That's different," said Millicent. "He pours coffee here. No one pays attention to the people who wait on them. It's the perfect cover, really. Coffee pourers. Busboys. Waiters. To most people, they're invisible."

"There is nothing about this boy that is invisible," said Aunt Emily.

"Do you know what will happen to this place if they find him?" asked Millicent. "There will be more paparazzi here than there are mosquitoes. Besides, when you mess up like that, sometimes you need time. He's not ready to go back."

Mess up like that. Another direct hit to the face.

"I want to go," Elvis said again. "I want to be Aaron."

Aunt Emily put her hands on his shoulders and they both faced Millicent. "See. He wants to be Aaron."

"Hey, Wonder Boy," said Millicent, "you do know that

Aaron is a kid we made up? Right? You know he's not real? And that he's a disguise for you while you're here?"

Aaron . . . er . . . Elvis nodded.

"He's going," announced Aunt Emily.

Millicent threw her hands up in the air. "Don't let anyone take your picture," she barked. "They might look at the picture and figure it out."

"If I see a camera, I'll duck."

"Don't tap your feet if there's music in the background. I've seen you do it. Even when you're just listening, you get lost in the song."

Elvis looked at Aunt Emily to see if this was true. Aunt Emily nodded. "Just like your dad did when he was your age. You know, he used to live in this town when we were both teenagers. It was before he even had his stage name. He wasn't Austin Ruby. His name was William Ruber then. You look a lot like him when you get lost in a song. I suppose Millicent is right," she said. "You should be a little careful. When you talk and when you laugh . . . well, you do have a way of lighting up a room."

It was his charisma, that magical quality that made people adore him. "I will try to be dull," he said. Deep down, he wondered if it was possible.

"Don't make eye contact. Look in a different direction."

He leaned down near the toaster and gazed at his reflection.

When you're filled with charisma the eyes will always give you away.

"Don't tell them you're from New York."

He nodded again.

"Don't tell them about your dad and sister or that you've traveled to every major city in the United States."

Something about the way that Millicent barked out her list of don'ts reminded Elvis of a military march, one with bossy horns and rapid-fire drums.

"One more thing," she said. "Cecilia has a dog. If you're stuck on a question, bend down to pet the dog. It will give you some time."

Aunt Emily patted him on the back. "You'll be fine. But for now, it's time to go to bed."

"One more thing," Millicent said again, but Elvis had the feeling that she'd be telling him "one more thing" until he went to Cecilia's house on Sunday. It would be a week of warnings.

My Name Is Elvis Ruby

That night Elvis tossed and turned. He wrestled with the sheets and he wrestled with Millicent's words. Finally he fell into a sleep deep enough to dream.

In his dream he didn't freeze on stage. In his dream he didn't *mess up like that*.

Instead, he stood behind the curtains. The host introduced him. His father and Cher held up their "We Love You, Elvis" signs, just like it happened in real life.

And he stepped into the white-hot lights, just like he did on the show.

While the audience cheered, he brimmed with star power. He oozed charisma. He was magnetic.

And he put his guitar on and he began to play.

In the dream he played every instrument he knew. The piano. The guitar. The violin. The flute. The drums. The ukulele. The horn. The harp.

But no matter how hard he sang, banged, strummed, blew, bowed, or drummed, no music came out. Nothing. There was only silence.

The audience bristled. The stage managers hissed. The judges whispered.

He tried everything. A jig. Some jazz. A cha-cha-cha. A hula.

Rock. Ragtime. Rap. Rumbas.

And every single song that Elvis Presley, the king of rock and roll, ever sang.

Hundreds of notes tumbled out of him. But they were all empty. Soundless.

It was the silence that jolted him awake. He sat up in bed, reeling from the weight of the dream. He hugged Fred.

He reached under the bed and felt around. Hidden underneath a pile of Millicent's photos of beaches, pineapples, and palm trees were some of his musical instruments. His father had pressed them into Aunt Emily's hands the night they arrived from New York.

He pulled out his flute and opened the latch on the case. Underneath the mouthpiece he found a crumpled piece of paper.

It was his *TweenStar* speech, the one that they ask the contestants to give onstage before they perform. "Even before they hear you sing, they'll hear you speak. This is where America decides if they love you, Elvis. We've got to make it sparkle," his father said. So together, they crafted every word.

"My name is Elvis Ruby," he read, half to himself, half out loud. "I can make a guitar wail. My blues are soulful. And when I play a happy tune on a violin old ladies spring to their feet and dance. I can rock. And rap. And my drumming has been called 'explosive.' And I can make a piano talk in seven different languages. On the flute I'm a regular Pied Piper. And when I sing, I'll make you think of memories you haven't had yet." He flipped the page over. There was more written on the other side. "My name is Elvis Ruby and I am a star!"

The first time he recited it, he received a standing ovation. The audience cheered. The press called it "pitch perfect" and "brilliant." By the following morning, it had been translated into seventeen different languages and had received over two million hits on YouTube.

After the speech, he played his violin and sang. From that moment he was catapulted from a musical boy who had a somewhat famous guitarist father to a major star. An instant celebrity. A rare combination of talent and charisma.

"This is what we worked so hard for. The cameras love you. The audience thinks you're amazing. There's no way you can lose," his father had told him over and over again. And the world agreed. They adored him.

Elvis folded the paper carefully, grabbed the flute, and headed down the hallway. He tiptoed past the couch where Millicent slept and hurried through the restaurant part of the Pancake Palace. He pushed the screen door open and slunk down the side steps into the back yard.

When he reached the trees, he patted the Old Man, rested by the Thief, and brushed a branch of Wandering Bill. It was always cooler beneath them.

Elvis placed the flute to his lips and blew.

A single whispery sound came out.

There was a flash of light near the woods.

He leaned into the shadows of the trees and watched.

When the light moved closer, Elvis dived for the ground.

Syncopated Beats

Elvis had to be tasting dirt, his face was pressed up so tight against the ground. He probably had a tiny mountain of the stuff rammed into his mouth.

Cecilia shone her flashlight at him. "What are you doing? Are you okay?" she asked, relieved to see he had taken a quick breath.

Elvis stood up. His hair was mussed. His face was dirty. There was nothing bright and starlike about him.

"I saw a flash. I thought it was a paparazzi camera." He paused, looking straight at her. "I thought you turned me in."

"Turned you in? You thought that?" She shone the light right in his eyes. "Really?"

He didn't answer. Instead, Elvis wiped his face with his

sleeve and spit on the ground. It was not exactly something she expected a superstar celebrity to do.

"Why are you here?" he asked. In the warm spring night, Elvis shivered.

Cecilia had come to tell him that RJ knew. It was Elvis's secret after all. He had a right to know who knew it. But when she saw him shiver, his face as pale as sugar sand, she didn't have the heart to tell. Besides, he already thought she'd turned him in. "I sneak out of the house and wander at night. I go to the edge of the woods. I listen for the song." At least she had told some of the truth.

"Every night?"

Cecilia picked up the flute from the ground and handed it to him. "That's why I need your help."

Elvis answered slowly. "If I don't do what you say, will you turn me in?"

And you know, for a second Cecilia was going to say yes. It was tempting. She'd never do it, of course, but how could Elvis be sure of that? All she'd have to do is threaten. She had his secret to hold over him. He'd go into the woods a hundred times to keep it.

He stood there, waiting for an answer, his face filthy, speckled with sand. "Please," he said in a very small voice. "I like being Aaron."

There was something humble and even a little pathetic

about the way he asked. And Cecilia remembered that night he'd cried.

She looked straight into his sandy face. "Then I will call you Aaron. And I won't tell."

Except for telling RJ, what Cecilia said was true.

What if RJ told? He would only do it accidentally, of course, but what if he slipped? Who would come to Wares Grove? Reporters? Paparazzi? Television crews? Screaming fans? Girls like Natalie Bracer and her crowd? Did they all have pink scrapbooks with his name scribbled on the cover?

She closed her eyes and imagined hundreds of Natalies standing outside the Pancake Palace screaming "Elvis! Oh, Elvis! I love you so!"

Her eyes popped open, then she stepped back and tripped. He caught her.

"Do you believe me? About the song?" she asked.

Of course he didn't. But he shrugged out of politeness.

"You're the most musical person I've ever met. If anyone would hear it, it would be you."

His specialness. It was going to get him in trouble again.

Cecilia pointed her flashlight at the edge of the woods. She grabbed his arm. "I have stood here for many nights and I have tried and tried. So tell me. Please. What would you do if you were listening for a song?"

She pulled him into the sugar-sand path. They took a few

hesitant steps on the path. But after a few twists and turns, Elvis stopped. The pine trees hung around him. "I guess the first thing I'd do is try to hear the beat."

"The beat?"

"Yeah. Like a rhythm. Most every place has one."

"Does New York City?" Cecilia asked. She had only been there once.

"Sure. New York City is easy. It sounds like people hurrying fast. And L.A. is almost the same. No. Maybe not. I guess it depends on what part of L.A. you're in. Trying to keep up with the beat of L.A. can make you dizzy even if you play fourteen instruments like I do."

"Philadelphia?" she asked.

"It sounds like a drum march. Very patriotic."

"Miami?"

Elvis began to move his feet. "That one is hot and tropical, like a tango."

She couldn't stump him. For every city, he had an answer.

"Detroit?"

"One that jangles like a tambourine."

"Sedona, Arizona?"

"Think of rain in the desert. A soothing beat."

"New Orleans?"

"New Orleans is my favorite. It's syncopated." Elvis did a hop. "Syncopated beats are filled with surprises. Instead of

ONE, two, three, four, you put the beat in the place that's not expected. One, TWO, three, four." Elvis clapped his hands in time with his beats. "One, TWO"—startled birds flew out of a nearby tree—"three, four. Can you hear the difference?"

Cecilia shrugged. "I'm not very musical."

Elvis clapped again. This time he motioned for her to clap with him. Instead Cecilia put her hands in her pockets. "Must be interesting . . ." she mused.

"To be famous? To be surrounded by thousands of fans?" Elvis finished her thought. It was a common interview question. Everyone wanted to know.

Cecilia shook her head. "To play music. To hear beats in cities. To know when something is syncopated."

"Before . . ." said Elvis. His life would always be divided into before he froze onstage and after. "I guess it felt the same for me as it does for everyone. You know when you hear a good song on the radio or TV or something and you're so filled up with it that you have to sing?"

"I'm not a singer."

"Well, everyone feels like they have to sing."

"Not everyone."

"But what about when you listen? You have to get filled up with a song then. My dad always says that the best part of being a musician is that moment of silence after you finish your song and before the audience starts to clap. That's the magical spot. When everyone is so filled up with the song you played that they can't even move."

Cecilia yanked at his arm. "Maybe we need to go a little farther down the path."

Elvis pulled away and began walking back in the direction of the Pancake Palace. "No. Let's turn around."

"Come on. There's safety in numbers. With two of us, we can do it. Nothing to be afraid of. You already said you can hear beats." Cecilia ran in front of him, trying to block his way. She tried to push him back in the other direction.

But Elvis stood as unmovable as a pine. "I can't. Not now."

Cecilia gave up pushing. Instead she went over to his other side and tried to pull.

"I don't have my violin," he protested.

"Oh." She paused for a second. "But look, you have your flute. Maybe that will work." She tugged again.

"I can't."

She tugged harder. "Why not?"

"I can't play." Elvis was breathing heavily. "Since that night onstage, I've tried. But nothing happens."

Cecilia scratched her head and then she pulled again. This time it was a two-handed tug. "Come on. The moment you hear the song, it will all come back to you. That's what happened to the fiddler Sammy Buck. He only heard it once. And he was able to play. He was musical, like you. Maybe you can listen to beats."

"There are no beats," he whispered.

"No beats? But you just finished saying that every place has one."

Elvis waved to the trees around him. "Not this place."

In protest, the night birds grew louder.

"Of course you don't hear it now. We have to go into the woods." Cecilia pulled so hard, her hands slipped. She landed on the ground.

She lay there on her back staring up at the stars.

It took Cecilia a while to realize that his outstretched hand was for her. She reached for him and Elvis pulled her up.

"There has to be something," Cecilia said, but before she could brush the sand from her clothes, Elvis had hurried away.

What the
Thief Caught

If she called him by a name, he might have stopped running. But Cecilia wasn't sure which one to use. She started with "Elvis," then she switched to "Aaron," so it came out "Elviiaaaron," which was hardly a name at all. Just a sound.

By the time she pried the flute from the branches of the Thief, Elvis was back inside the Pancake Palace. The light that had been on in Millicent's room was out. The place was dark.

He must have thrown the flute as he ran.

She poked around more with her flashlight. The beam caught something else, a crumpled paper trapped between some twigs.

In big bold letters were the words "My name is Elvis Ruby and I am a star!"

She flipped it over. There was more on the other side. When she got to the part that said "make you think of memories you haven't had yet," she closed it up and held it tight.

The Pygmy Forest

Somewhere in the middle of the next night, Elvis heard a rap on the window. Cecilia called his name. He kicked off his blankets, tossed Fred under the bed, and peeked outside.

She stood near the Palace wall and spoke in a voice that was way too loud for nighttime. "I've got it all figured out."

Elvis glanced back into the house. "Shhh. They're sleeping. You don't want to wake up Aunt Emily and especially not Millicent."

But even the threat of Millicent didn't quiet Cecilia down. "I know why I never heard the song," she shouted. "Bring your flute. I know you have it. I left it on your back steps last night."

Elvis crossed his arms in front of him. "No flute."

"Okay. Fine. But please come down." Her voice grew louder, more impatient.

In the end it was the fear of Millicent waking up that made him climb out the window. Before he had his two feet on the ground, Cecilia was shouting, waving her flashlight, and brandishing a big stick. "We need to be on the banks of the cedar swamp stream. That's where my parents were. That's where I was born. I bet that's where it hides." She squinted her eyes. "Isn't that where you'd hide if you were a song?"

"Hide? How would I know?" Elvis was used to questions like this. When you're famous, people expect you to have all the answers.

"Well, you're the musical one. Not me." Cecilia moved around a little, pressing her stick into the ground with each step she took.

"What's that for?"

"Snakes. If you're walking at night, you put the stick in front of you so you don't run into snakes. Black snakes, pine snakes, garden snakes—they're all okay. But you don't want to run into a copperhead or a rattler."

Elvis picked each foot up and checked the ground around him. Then he peered over at the low clumps of bushes, eyeing them all suspiciously.

"The problem is the cedar swamp is dark even on sunny days. I can't imagine what it's like at night. Plus, I'm not sure I know how to get there." She looked out at the trees. "In the daytime, I know what paths to follow, but things are always different at night." She pulled his arm. "Let's go."

Elvis backed away. "On a path filled with snakes?"

"It's not filled with snakes. There's an occasional snake."

"I've never even been in the woods in the daylight."

"Never?"

"City streets. Parking lots of stadiums and concert halls. Dark alleys. I'm your guy for those things." He flashed his famous smile.

"Then we'll go this weekend. After my birthday celebration. At least you can see the swamp stream during the day." Cecilia grabbed his hand. "Come with me. I want to show you something."

He followed her, keeping close. They traveled down a sandy path to where the pines were short and mangled. "It's called a pygmy forest. Those trees won't grow much taller than you. And it's kind of special. You're looking at the largest pygmy forest on this earth. Hundreds of miles of it. That's why we don't want to make any wrong turns on our way to the cedar swamp," Cecilia said. "And it sure looks different when it's dark."

The second night after Cecilia rapped on his window and he hurried out, they went a little farther into the woods.

By the third night, he was waiting for her with a bag of Palace leftovers. They wandered down the paths, nibbling on pancakes, and Elvis decided he liked the Whites the best. Cecilia led the way. She checked for snakes and pointed out wildlife. Owls. Raccoons. A nest of birds.

He was finishing up the last of the pancakes when there was a crunch nearby. And then another. Footsteps. Movement. "It's a deer, probably. They're all over the place," Cecilia whispered. "Anytime you go out into the woods at night, you can hear them. Something's always around. It's kind of nice, isn't it?"

Elvis looked into the woods and whispered, "Not when you're worried about being followed."

A Musical Interlude

If you go into the Pinelands without stopping at the Pancake Palace and head down a sandy path to where the old-timers live, you might hear a different version of that Jersey Devil story. The part everyone knows, of course, is that a baby was born hundreds of years ago on a stormy December night in a house with a leaky roof and an ill-tempered mother. Before he took his first breath, his mother cried out, "I'm tired of children, let this one be the Devil." And most will say that it happened right away. But a few old-timers will tell you that he would never have flown out that chimney if it weren't for his six-year-old sister, Anna.

After he was born and his mother left him on that bed, it was Anna who reached for him first. She wrapped him in a blanket and begged him not to become what their mother had said. But when Anna felt the two hard bumps on the top of his head and saw a tiny growth on his shoulder blades, she knew.

Three days later when Anna saw how he had changed, she cradled him in her arms and covered him tight. "You can't stay here. They'll never let you." But there were so many children in that leaky little house that no one noticed the new baby had grown horns and wings, and he didn't see the point in flying away just yet. Instead he nestled deeper into Anna's arms.

So she told him about the song. "The Pinelands has a music all its own. And once when I was out there alone, I heard it. And it was the most beautiful sound I'd ever heard." And she hummed a few bars so he'd know it was true. He said goodbye in his eyes, thought Anna. Then he flew away.

It was the promise of the music that sent him into the pines. And ever since that morning, he's been out there too, a poor unfortunate devil in search of that song.

Everyone's Brother

The next day after the lunch dishes were cleared and the tables were set for the dinner rush, Aunt Emily pulled Elvis aside. "Here's where you learn the family secret," she said.

More secrets. He turned away.

Millicent put her hand on his shoulder. "Consider yourself lucky. I was fourteen before she showed me how she does this and I'm her daughter."

He tried to squirm away.

"Hey, Wonder Boy," she said. "Why are you trying to run? Don't you want to learn how to make the pancakes?"

Elvis never cooked. Neither did his dad or Cher. They were on the road too much. Before he went on *TweenStar*, they traveled from one concert to the next. If they were home, it was takeout. House of Wong, the Shake Shack, Harriet's Kitchen, and Murray's Sturgeon Shop were all listed as favorites on his dad's cell phone.

But he was incognito now. He was no longer Elvis Ruby. He was Aaron. And that meant he could be a cook. Not an expert. Aaron, he decided, would not be an expert in anything. Aaron was going to be a Doc Bashful boy, the most average boy in the state of New Jersey. A kid you'd forget. A kid no one was expecting greatness from.

Regular boys would know how to make regular food, like pancakes. They'd use spatulas and spoons and bowls. They'd crack eggs and sift flour. For some reason, Elvis Ruby always imagined regular boys sifting flour.

"Yes, please. Show me how? Can I sift?"

Millicent grabbed the eggs and the milk while Aunt Emily got out the flour. They worked in a rhythm, stopping only to call out the amounts.

"Three eggs," said Millicent.

"Three cups of flour," Aunt Emily shot back. "And yes, you can sift."

Aaron sifted, not too expertly. It was very average sifting.

"Two tablespoons baking powder." Millicent snapped the spoon against the bowl each time she measured a spoonful. It sounded like a shallow drum.

"Never put the flour in all at once," warned Aunt Emily.

"You need to take it slow and mix it in," said Millicent. "Or you'll get lumps."

"And now for the supersecret ingredient." Aunt Emily waved her spoon like a wand.

"Almond flavoring," Millicent jumped in before Aunt Emily had a chance.

"Just a drop. You can't really tell what it is when it's mixed in, but it adds an extra depth and flavor to the batter." Aunt Emily ran her hand under water and then flicked it over the grill. "Here's how you know you have the right temperature."

The water skittered around the surface.

"See how the water dances on the griddle?" said Aunt Emily. "When the water gets like that, you can pour the batter."

Millicent flicked some more water over the grill. It danced again. "It's called the Leidenfrost effect," she said. "When things get too hot, the water forms beads and jumps around instead of evaporating."

"My daughter the librarian had to look that up," said Aunt Emily.

"Yep. Someday soon, maybe I'll be a librarian with a job." Millicent swayed her hips like a hula dancer.

Aunt Emily laughed. "Remember the first time you made pancakes, Milllicent? You mixed them for so long that they came out hard as hockey pucks."

"We tried to feed them to the squirrels, but even they didn't want them."

Aunt Emily laughed, but when she poured the pancake batter onto the grill she turned serious. "This part is important. As soon as you pour the batter onto the pan, that's when you put in your blueberries and cranberries. Some chefs mix the berries into the batter"—she gave an exaggerated shiver—"but I would never."

Elvis flipped the pancakes. When the blueberries hit the heat, they spit out juice.

"Remember, the only people who know about the almond flavoring are in this kitchen." Aunt Emily put her hands on his shoulders.

"So keep it a secret, okay?" said Millicent.

Now, even the pancakes had secrets.

Perhaps it was the way Millicent said it or the word itself, but Elvis slunk away. How many secrets could one boy handle?

The screen door opened. Three girls his age walked in. He grabbed some menus and place mats. They had customers.

The first girl ordered coffee. Black. No sugar. She smiled at Aaron like he should be impressed at her grown-up beverage choice. He wasn't. Her two friends ordered lemonade.

"You look familiar," said the coffee girl. She smelled like raspberries.

The others nodded. And all three of them looked him up and down. It made him run his hands over his hair and stare at the ground.

"I'm a regular guy who looks like everyone else," he said, and he immediately realized his mistake. Regular guys do not say they look like regular guys.

One of the lemonade girls smiled. It was a flirty smile. He remembered them from his Elvis Ruby days.

He turned away, but the coffee drinker wasn't about to let him go. "What school do you go to?" she asked.

"I'm not from around here."

"But I *know* you."

"She's right. You look very familiar," said one of the lemonade girls.

"Doubt it," he mumbled.

Way in the back by the pancake grill, Aunt Emily began to hum. He glanced around for Millicent, who never seemed to be around when he needed her.

The coffee girl grabbed his arm. Her purple-polished nails dug into him. Shy Violet. That was the name of the color she was wearing. At *TweenStar*, all the girls used it. He had even done a commercial for the company, a thirty-second spot. He sang while a contestant named Jasmeen played the piano. There were lots of close-ups of Jasmeen's fingers. At the end of the spot, they stood next to each other, facing the camera. Jasmeen held up her nails and said, "The only thing shy about me is my nail color." It was his job to smile.

"Seriously, you look familiar." The girl relaxed her grip only a little.

"I remind everyone of their brother." Yes, that was it. Aaron would be like everyone's brother, the regular guy who was sometimes fun to be with, sometimes annoying, and sometimes you didn't even notice he was there. He kept his voice dull. Monotone. Nothing to let the charisma ooze out. Aaron wouldn't have an ounce of charisma.

"I don't have a brother." The coffee girl downed her coffee and pointed to her empty cup.

"Me neither," said her friend.

"I do and you're nothing like him," said the third.

It took three songs before they left. A Swedish folk song. An accordion solo. And a zippy tune by the yodeling cowboy, Sourdough Slim.

"Come on," the coffee girl shouted over Sourdough Slim's high-pitched "yaaaaa-deeeee-ooooos," "there's that Lost Treasures store across the street. I want to see what I can buy."

Elvis took his first deep breath when the door closed tight behind them.

Hiding Out Near the Toilet Seats

Across the street and down the road a little, Cecilia could smell Natalie Bracer's signature raspberry bubblegum scent the moment she and her two friends walked into the Lost Treasures Thrift and Throwaway Store.

"It'll only be a few minutes, I just want to look around," she heard Natalie say.

Cecilia scooted past the blue jeans, all lined up in size order, and the used books, scattered every which way, and the wooden ninja sword that said "Sal's Martial Arts Supply Company," and hid behind the boxes of toilet seats, which Mrs. Herbert assured her were not secondhand at all but brand-new, just the wrong color.

"I don't want to shop here." It was the voice of Natalie's best friend, Reeza Blu. "This place is creepy."

"Stores like this are the only place to find things that are different. I like wearing clothes that are vintage," Natalie said.

Cecilia never used the word "vintage" to describe a purchase from the Lost Treasures Thrift and Throwaway Store, but since it was the only store in Wares Grove, she shopped there all the time.

Suddenly the worn hem of her periwinkle T-shirt didn't seem so bad. Mrs. Herbert knew it was her favorite color and put it aside for her the moment it came in. "It's vintage," she practiced saying softly to herself in case someone ever asked.

"Can I help you girls?" she heard Mrs. Herbert say.

Instead of answering, Natalie and her friends giggled.

"Well, you just let me know if you need any help." Mrs. Herbert's voice grew brisk.

Cecilia could hear Mrs. Herbert's heavy steps walking up and down the aisles. If she stayed tucked away in her spot, she could hide until the girls were gone.

Slow footsteps came her way. "There you are," said Mrs. Herbert. "I found what I wanted to show you." She held a pen with a clear top. Inside the pen cap was a liquid that had a pink Cadillac floating inside it. "For your floaty pen collection. How many do you have now?"

Cecilia had no choice but to stand tall next to the boxes

of toilet seats, which were brand-new, but still, it would have been so much better to be sighted next to the perfume bottles or hair clips. She waved at Natalie and the others. None of them waved back.

Cecilia pretended she didn't notice. "I have over a hundred," she said, trying to keep the quiver from her voice.

"This one is a souvenir from the city of Memphis. It says so on the side." Mrs. Herbert pointed to the fancy script. "Look, it says, 'Memphis, the Birthplace of Rock and Roll.' I bet you didn't know that." Mrs. Herbert handed it to Cecilia, and Cecilia shoved it into her pocket without even looking at it.

"Floaty pens," Natalie Bracer whispered to the other girls and all three of them smirked.

It wasn't like Cecilia wanted to be friends with Natalie. All she wanted was to wave and have them wave back. And not have them smirk or explode into giggly whispers, like they were now.

Mrs. Herbert pointed her knobby finger at Natalie. "I know your dad. Before I worked here, I was a teacher. Your father was in my sixth-grade class. You look just like him. You have his mouth and his eyes."

Then she turned to the girl standing beside her. "I had almost forty years in that school district, which means I also taught your grandfather. His name is Peter, right?"

The giggling whispers stopped. "My mom should be

outside now. She's waiting for us in the car," said the girl whose grandfather's name was Peter. She tugged at Natalie's arm, anxious to get out.

The three girls bumped into each other on their way out the door and exploded into more giggles.

As soon as they left, Mrs. Herbert said, "Try not to pay attention to them. There will always be girls like Natalie and her friends."

"She's very pretty," said Cecilia, picking up a braided silver chain and holding it in her hands. "Natalie stands out because she's pretty."

Mrs. Herbert took the chain, unlocked the clasp, and put it around Cecilia's neck. "She's pretty now, I suppose. She's still young. She'll lose her looks by the time she's sixteen. All the Bracer kids do." Then she held up a mirror so Cecilia could see. "And you will continue to shine from within."

Cecilia smiled at Mrs. Herbert. It was a very nice thing for an old lady to say to a young girl. But never in her life had Cecilia felt shiny.

Beyond the Yodels

Elvis listened to the music of the yodeling cowboy for the rest of the afternoon. But all the Sourdough Slim songs in the world couldn't yodel away the fact that those girls came close to discovering who he was. He could tell by the way that coffee girl grabbed his arm and by the flirty smile from that lemonade girl. They were moments away from recognizing him.

And what if they did? How would they react? It was different before he froze onstage. He knew what would have happened before.

Before, his fans would wait outside in the cold or the rain, screaming his name, holding up painted signs they spent hours making. But after the big freeze, the people who stood outside his apartment were paparazzi with mega-huge cameras trying to snap a picture for the front page of a gossip magazine and reporters who shouted out questions like "How does it feel to have let down your adoring fans?" or "How did you feel when that *TweenStar* judge called you a disappointment to America and the entire rest of the world?"

And his adoring fans? Some of them shouted things like "We *still* love you," but he stopped reading his fan mail because too many letters started with words like "You broke my heart."

He was Elvis Ruby, disappointment to his fans, to America, and to the entire rest of the world.

Being Aaron was definitely a better choice.

The walls felt close. The air felt thick, like blueberry syrup. It was hard to breathe.

Elvis mumbled to Aunt Emily that he was leaving and then headed out the back door. He ran down the steps and into the woods. Cecilia was right. It was different in the daylight. He traveled down the sugar-sand path and into the pygmy forest. Crooked limbs grabbed at him, like anxious fans after he gave a concert.

Elvis tried to remember the last time he was alone. It had been months. In *TweenStar* the contestants were always in groups. And even if he did happen to be by himself, there were always the cameras. For the entire television season, the contestants lived in the *TweenStar* mansion and there were cameras everywhere. Every move they made was watched by millions. It was a reality show after all.

Before that, he traveled on a crowded tour bus with his father, Cher, and the rest of the band. He was hardly ever alone.

With Sourdough Slim yodeling in the distance, Elvis was free to explore.

If he followed the yodels, he'd find his way back. The "yaa-deee-oooos" filled up the trees.

He took a few more steps. The paths grew smaller. The trees grew tighter together. A hawk circled overhead.

Sourdough Slim and his yodels were getting farther and farther away. But Elvis heard something else coming from the opposite direction. Music. He could tell what instrument it was by the first note. A violin. Or maybe it was a bird that sounded like a violin? It was hardly a tune at all, only a few scrambled notes.

No, this was no bird. He was certain of it. Someone was playing a violin.

He listened again, but the sound was gone.

Karaoke

The next day at school Mrs. Montañez announced to Cecilia and the rest of her class that they had a substitute teacher for music. "I'm sorry to say that Mrs. Putnam is out today. I'm afraid she's going to be out for a few days."

Cecilia was not surprised. Mrs. Putnam suffered from migraines that she described as pounders. And then there was her bad knee that always gave her trouble. "Your music teacher today will be Mr. Kring. He has something very special planned."

"Dudes," said Mr. Kring, and he was the first teacher in the entire school who ever called them dudes. "We're going to have a talent show. You're all going to be in it."

Natalie Bracer and her friends nudged each other and

grinned. "If his teeth were a little whiter, he'd almost look like Zander Fox, the host of *TweenStar*," whispered Natalie. She pushed her bangs out of her face.

TweenStar. Cecilia looked down at her desk, hiding her grin. If Natalie Bracer only knew.

"Will there be judges?" asked Reeza Blu. She nudged Natalie's arm and Natalie nudged her back.

"No worries, dudes, I wouldn't do that to you. No mean judges here." Mr. Kring flashed a smile. Not exactly the whitest-teeth-in-America smile, but still it was impressive. "So today, I'll put you in groups. I'll have a bunch of you stand up and sing. Then next week, we'll perform on a stage."

Mr. Kring put a song on a machine. "It's a karaoke machine. Justin Bieber. Taylor Swift. I've got all the good songs here."

The class cheered, except for Cecilia, who stared at Mr. Kring's Adam's apple. It bobbed up and down when he spoke.

Mr. Kring pressed the play button, and the class nodded their heads in time to the beat.

"Good song," said Tiffany Craw.

Cecilia traced the pen marks that were etched into her desk. There were horns. Some drums. But something about the song sounded sharp and jagged, like the noise in her father's workshop when he dropped the container of nails and they fell to the ground all at once.

Mr. Kring played another song.

"My favorite!" said Reeza Blu. She tapped her foot in time with the beat.

"Like it?" asked Mr. Kring.

Everyone except Cecilia shouted back, "Yes!"

"See how you're all bobbing up and down?" Mr. Kring said. "That is the magic of music. You have to move to the rhythm."

Cecilia tapped her foot. But when she looked at the others in the class, she could see she was horribly out of beat.

RJ was in the group that went up first. So was Natalie's best friend, Reeza Blu.

As soon as Mr. Kring put on their karaoke song, they began to sing. They swayed together. They all stepped to the right. Then they all stepped to the left. And they clapped. They sang. They laughed.

"Great song!" said RJ.

"Awesome!" said Reeza.

RJ and Reeza high-fived before they sat down again.

And Cecilia tried to put it out of her mind that RJ had just high-fived Reeza, who was never really nice to her.

She tried to catch his eye, but RJ seemed too interested in the music to be thinking about much else. He drummed his fingers on his desk.

Mr. Kring pressed his hands together and closed his eyes

like he was lost in solemn prayer. "Don't you love it when a beat and melody come together?"

The class nodded.

Mr. Kring called her name. "Come on up, Cecilia Wreel. It's time for you and the Craw twins to show us what you've got." He said it in a television announcer's voice. The class giggled.

Taffy and Tiffany Craw hurried to the front of the classroom. Even before Mr. Kring put on the music, the Craw girls were singing.

The voices. The notes. They rattled around Cecilia like that box of nails. The rest of the kids clapped in time to the beat.

"Ah, the golden voices of the Craw twins. I've heard about you two. You perform at Albert Hall sometimes, don't you?" said Mr. Kring when they finished their song.

Taffy and Tiffany nodded.

"Your harmonizing is lovely," he said. And the class cheered.

"Cecilia." Mr. Kring waved. "Join them."

Cecilia looked behind her. Perhaps another girl with the name Cecilia would appear in the back of the room. And that new girl would know how to move in time to the beat. She would know the names of the songs and she would know how to sing. But there was only one Cecilia in the entire school, much less the fifth grade.

"Do you know that Cecilia is the name of the patron saint of music?" said Mr. Kring.

Cecilia nodded. "I was almost Ashley. But my parents changed their minds at the last minute." There were over a dozen Ashleys in her school and Cecilia adored that name for its commonness.

Mr. Kring was standing by her desk when she looked up. "Come on, don't be shy." He was still smiling but barely.

Cecilia rubbed her throat. "I have a cold."

"You were fine this morning," said Natalie, giving Mr. Kring a brilliant smile.

"It's okay, Cecilia," said Taffy Craw. "Come sing with us."

But Cecilia only put her head down on the desk, and Mr. Kring moved on to his next victim.

You Can't Escape It

Later that afternoon, Elvis watched Cecilia from the window of the Pancake Palace. It was the fifth time she had walked by since she got off the school bus. Each time she circled closer and closer to the front porch. But even so, he jumped a little bit when the screen door snapped open.

Cecilia sank into a chair. Her eyes were puffy and moist. Something about the way she slumped reminded him of Cher when she got into one of her moods.

He handed her a menu, but she waved it away.

"Blues," she sniffed. "A short stack."

Before he dropped off her order, he stopped at the music pile and searched for a song. He knew exactly which one to pick. A song with playful ukuleles and a happy tropical beat would be just the thing to make her happy.

Aunt Emily peeked out from behind her griddle. "Here," she whispered. "I gave her a few extra." The stack was piled so high that one wrong move would send them tumbling. Pancakes get cold fast, and they're never as good as when they're hot and steamy. So Elvis hurried.

Elvis placed the plate in front of Cecilia with the same flourish that waiters used at the finest restaurants. Then he did a quick and quiet dance, taking tiny steps from side to side. "The last time I played this song Aunt Emily and Millicent sang and danced the hula." Elvis grinned. "Those two can get really goofy when there are no customers around."

Cecilia pressed her hands into her face and sniffled.

"What's wrong? What's making you upset? Is it the song? You don't like the song?" After all these weeks of chasing out customers by knowing what songs people liked and didn't like, he was sure he'd picked a winner.

"Not much," she blurted out.

Elvis changed the song to one his father always played at the end of a concert. "Everyone likes this one. It's old-time rock and roll. Remember I told you about how syncopated beats are my favorites? You can hear it in this song. Listen. Hear how it's completely unexpected and filled with surprises? It's the beat that walks you through the song."

"Yeah, yeah," Cecilia murmured, polite, but nothing else.

"You don't like this one either? Well, what would you like? Something you can dance to? Something that makes you feel quiet on the inside?"

"I don't want any."

"No music? It always helps me. You need something to cheer you up. What's your favorite?"

"None."

"You have to like something."

Cecilia shoved her fork into a pancake and shrugged.

"That can't be," he said. "Everyone likes some type of music."

"I am not musical," she sniffed. "I have given up even trying to sing. When it comes to dancing, I have two left feet." That was the expression she heard her first-grade teacher whisper to her parents. "Two left feet." It was after the school play where she and Natalie Bracer were the only two girls cast as dancing flower buds. Before they went onstage, Natalie Bracer had actually hugged her. As soon as the music started, Cecilia skipped when she should have hopped. Turned instead of skipped. The audience laughed and Natalie Bracer never forgave her for messing up.

Elvis sat down next to her.

Cecilia waved her hand around the room. "And, you know, it's everywhere. Stores. Schools. Churches. Cars. You can't escape it."

"Why would you want to escape it?" he asked.

Cecilia extracted a blueberry from deep inside a pancake and popped it into her mouth. "You know, when you're not singing the right notes and you join in, people stare at you."

The song ended. Another one came on. Elvis drummed his fingers in time to the new beat. "You just haven't found the type of music you like," he said. "I can help you. We'll go through every single song if we have to. I've got a huge collection here."

The bell on the front door rang. Andrea and Jack Blades hurried in with Jack Junior, who even though he had yet to touch the maple syrup already had a messy, sticky face.

"Just sit wherever you want." Aunt Emily's voice rang out from the back.

Andrea and Jack sat down at the table by the window. Jack Junior stood in the middle of the room, closed his eyes, and spun like a top, around in circles. He banged into some chairs. They crashed to the ground.

Elvis picked up the chairs and brought the Blades their menus. "Tall stacks are extra tall today."

When he got back to Cecilia, her face was still pressed into her hands.

Elvis sat down beside her. "So if you don't like music, why do you want to go into the woods and hear that song?"

Cecilia looked up. "That's my last hope. *That* one has to be different."

What Would Aaron Like?

The day of Cecilia's birthday, Elvis walked down the street trying his best to remember all of Millicent's rules. As he had suspected, she went on for the whole week.

"Remember," she warned, "don't do anything that will make you stand out. Don't dance. Don't sing. Don't flash your winning smile. Don't talk about exotic foods, European castles, mansions, limousines, or fashion. Never mention music, parts of a song, parts of an instrument, parts of a musical production, parts of a stage, parts of a television show, or parts of a concert. If anyone else does, look away. Look up. Look down. Look sideways. Don't make eye contact. And, above all things, watch those Elvis Ruby gestures."

As soon as he turned up the walkway, Cecilia stepped out of the house. The screen door slammed behind her.

Something tugged at his shoelaces. "That's Storm," she explained.

He bent down near the picket fence and the dog sniffed his hand. "Does he bite?"

"No. But he will not be ignored," Cecilia said, and to prove this point, Storm pulled at Elvis's shoelaces so hard that they came untied. Cecilia watched Elvis tie his shoes and laughed when Storm pulled at them again. "He's a double dapple dachshund. Try to say *that* three times fast. It's very hard."

Of course, he could say "double dapple dachshund" three times fast. Speech lessons were all part of the *TweenStar* experience. The teacher had taken him aside to work on his pronunciation and diction. "Only use your tough New York accent for special occasions," she said. "Otherwise you must learn to speak without it. Accentless speech is the language of the superstars."

"Double dapple dachshund," he said, carefully pronouncing every—single—word.

"Faster," she demanded.

When he tried, she laughed.

"Most dachshunds are a single color," Cecilia explained. "See the spots. That means he's dappled. And he has white spots, which only happen if his father and mother were both dappled. So he's double dappled."

"He's cute," said Elvis.

"And bossy," said Cecilia.

Elvis pulled a CD out of his back pocket. "Here. I made this for you. I gave you music without any lyrics. Sometimes the words muddy things up. It's easier to listen to it without them."

"But I . . ." She didn't know what to say.

"These are my favorites. We'll listen to them together. We'll find something you like."

Cecilia nodded. "Come on, come meet my parents and Uncle Frank. You'll like Uncle Frank. Everyone does."

When Cecilia introduced him to her mom and dad, he mumbled. When Mrs. Wreel spoke, he stared down at her shoe. Fortunately, there are many eleven-year-old boys who happen to be shoe starers, so Mrs. Wreel thought it was a perfectly normal thing to do.

Mr. Wreel and Cecilia's uncle Frank shook his hand, and he glanced away.

"Okay, let's get this party started," said Mr. Wreel. "We've got some fancy appetizers." And Cecilia and her parents went into the kitchen to get the snacks.

Uncle Frank had an easy laugh. No wonder everyone liked him. He was loaded with charisma.

"So what do you do for fun, Aaron?" he asked, the moment the two were alone. "Sports? Books? Cooking? Fishing?" His questions came out rat-a-tat-tat. "Art? Skateboarding? Camping? Hunting? Music?"

Uncle Frank pointed to a guitar tucked in the corner of the living room right behind the magazine stand. It wasn't like Elvis hadn't noticed it before. The moment he walked in the room, he caught himself moving toward it. Instinct.

"What do I do for fun?" Elvis repeated the question, trying to buy himself some time.

The dog. The dog would give him a chance to think. He bent down and called for Storm. He even made the same clicking noise that Cecilia made.

"Yes. Fun?" Uncle Frank tapped on the chair, waiting for an answer.

Storm waddled by on his way to the kitchen, never even giving Elvis half a glance.

If he said music, it would get him into dangerous territory. Besides, Elvis never thought of music as something he did for fun. Playing music was like having a right and left hand. It just was.

Books. He was a reader. But it was mentioned in articles during the show. It was common knowledge.

What would Aaron like? The boy he was pretending to be. What would a boy with unstylish, short, choppy, sandy-colored hair who was a cousin of Aunt Emily's ex-husband and coming to the Pinelands for a visit do for fun?

"Sports," he mumbled out loud. Aaron would like sports.

Uncle Frank leaned toward him. "Do you play? Soccer? Little League? Wrestling? Or do you watch? Yankees? Mets? Phillies? Eagles? Fliers? Sixers? Giants?"

Elvis shrugged at every question. He should never have said sports. They were more complicated than he thought.

The doorbell rang and Cecilia was filled with worries. It would be the first time RJ saw Aaron since she blurted.

"Hi, Aaron," RJ said in a big voice. Then under his breath he whispered to Cecilia, "I hope you don't mind that I brought my mom." He made no mention of his thirteen-year-old sister, Elizabeth, who followed both of them into the living room.

"The more the merrier," said Mr. Wreel, and he hurried to set two more places at the table.

"Why is Elizabeth here?" Cecilia whispered.

"She wanted to come to say hi." RJ shrugged.

"She's never really done that before," Cecilia said. "In all my life, it's never happened."

And Elizabeth didn't break her streak. Instead, she plopped herself on the couch next to Elvis. "Welcome to New Jersey, Aaron," she said.

Cecilia pulled RJ over to the side. "Your sister's eyelashes fluttered." She pointed her finger at them.

"Her eyelashes never flutter," RJ said.

"And she just said, 'Welcome to New Jersey,'" said Cecilia, keeping her voice low. "Who says that?"

"So. She was being nice."

"She's *hardly ever* nice."

"Sometimes she's nice."

"Well, sometimes she's nice. But she's nice in her own Elizabeth way. Not in an eye-fluttery way. She's not 'Welcome to New Jersey' nice."

Where were the yawns? The eye rolls? The sarcastic comments? The one-word T-shirts that said things like "Later" and "Whatever"? Everything Cecilia knew Elizabeth to be was gone, replaced by this eye-fluttering, dressed-up version of RJ's sister.

Cecilia grabbed RJ by the shirt. She looked him straight in the eye. "Did you tell?"

RJ didn't answer. Instead he squatted down and called for the dog. Storm waddled toward him, his tail wagging. RJ leaned down low to the floor and let him bathe his face with licks.

A Narrow Escape

After those months in the *TweenStar* **mansion,** Elvis was used to birthday celebrations with crowds of celebrities and reporters, and waiters with silver trays of fancy food. And ice sculptures. And mountains of carefully decorated cupcakes. And fountains of chocolate. He could always find his friend Ramon near the chocolate. At one party, Ramon dipped everything into the fountain. The fancy sandwiches. The shrimp balls. The baby pizzas. "Everything but my bass guitar is better with chocolate," he said. The paparazzi loved it.

Before *TweenStar*, birthdays with his dad and Cher meant going to a restaurant with the entire stage crew and the band in whatever city they happened to be playing. When he turned nine, they ended up in Topeka, at a restaurant where they were served dinner in a coconut.

This was his first house party. Once during *TweenStar* he heard one of the contestants talk about spending a birthday at home with her mother and father and a few friends, before her father moved to the other side of town. She called it her "best birthday ever." Back then, it was something he couldn't even imagine doing.

Elvis snacked on cheese and crackers. And potato chips. And pork rolls, salty fried ham served on a bun. When he reached for seconds, Mrs. Wreel asked, "Have you ever had these before?"

Elvis shook his head.

"I'll remember you like them for the next time you come over, Aaron," said Mrs. Wreel. "But don't forget to save some room for dinner."

Suddenly *Aaron* had a favorite food. Pork rolls.

Mr. Wreel cleared away the snack tray, and Elvis offered to help. Aaron, he decided, would be polite.

Uncle Frank told a funny story. And Elvis laughed. *Aaron* should have a sense of humor. Besides, he was sitting next to Elizabeth and she was nice.

RJ moaned about a book report due Monday, and Elvis chimed in, "Sounds like fun."

The room grew silent.

Cecilia and RJ glanced at each other. Elizabeth smiled.

Cecilia's mom beamed. "A boy who likes homework."

"Math. Science. Spelling. I can't get enough of the stuff." Then to drive his point into the ground, he added, "Bring it on."

No kid would want to be known as the "boy who likes homework." Aaron, he decided, would have a dark side.

They had to think Aaron was real now.

Cecilia's mom and dad served the food. Mashed potatoes. Chicken. Salad. Coleslaw. And a steaming bowl of brussels sprouts. "These are Cecilia's favorites," Mrs. Wreel said as she put some on his plate.

It's funny how a little green ball of bitterness can change everything.

Elvis Ruby hated brussels sprouts and everyone knew. It made headlines. One careless comment to a reporter started everything. Nutritionists went on television to talk about the eating habits of America's youth. At *TweenStar* they called it negative press. When you're famous, the tiniest misstep can turn into a big event. The brussels sprouts comment had turned into a national media frenzy.

His "blech" face. It was a simple gesture that could get him found out.

RJ and Elizabeth glanced his way. He smiled at them and

pushed a brussels sprout onto his fork before he ate anything else. He chewed, smiling, resisting the urge to spit it out and grab his glass of water.

"Do you like them?" asked RJ's mom.

They were worse than he remembered. "Delicious," he lied.

Elizabeth dropped her fork.

And Aaron was left to grapple with that horrible taste in his mouth.

But he had done it. He was Aaron. Homework-loving. Brussels sprouts–eating. Regular kid.

He was safe.

Until RJ said, "Hey, let's sing 'Happy Birthday.' "

Cecilia jumped in quick. "No. There's no need. We haven't had cake yet. And my dad is going to tell the story."

RJ groaned.

"Whenever you're ready for it, honey," said Mr. Wreel, but he was deep in a conversation with Uncle Frank about lawn mowers.

"I can get the cake if you want," said her mom.

"No, not yet," protested Cecilia.

RJ had started already. He belted out the first lines by himself.

Elizabeth leaned over to Elvis and whispered, "You'll have to forgive my brother. He gets weird sometimes." Then she smiled. "But he's right. Maybe we should sing?" She fluttered her eyes. "Do you sing?"

If they sang, he'd be in trouble. In a party this size, everyone would notice if he didn't. Elizabeth would notice. She was sitting close to him.

He'd have to disguise his voice. He could make it squeaky and mouselike. Or he could sing the song like it was an opera, filled with brilliant falsettos. Or he could lower his voice till it croaked and sing notes loud and off-key.

What if he took shallow breaths? Singing is all about breath. It would go against his training and his instincts, but he could do it. He'd watched enough bad singers in his time. He knew how. If he didn't fill up his lungs until his stomach pouched out, if he only took a quick gasp, then his voice would sound faded and dull. He would try. He would reach for all the wrong notes. He would make all of the newbie-singer mistakes. It would be awful.

But would his bad singing be bad enough?

He was as famous for his voice as he was for his talents as a musician. A single trademark Elvis Ruby note and it would all be over.

RJ began the song for the seventh time.

Cecilia threw a napkin at him, and for a moment he was quiet.

Elvis reached under the table to pet Storm, but he was over

near Cecilia, begging for table scraps. It seemed his charisma didn't work on animals.

"Come on, Aaron," said Elizabeth. "Let's sing."

He was trapped.

"Headache!" Elvis shouted more like it was the answer to a question on a quiz show than like a person who was actually in pain. He rubbed his temples, thanked the Wreels for dinner, and ran out the door.

Being Aaron wasn't going to be as easy as he thought. There would always be land mines he'd have to tiptoe through and risk getting blown up. Like sports questions and brussels sprouts. And "Happy Birthday" songs.

He couldn't keep faking headaches. He'd have to think of another way.

He was almost back at the Pancake Palace when he realized that he'd left before Cecilia's dad told that story about the song.

A Disappointment

When Aaron got home, Aunt Emily and Millicent were sitting on the front porch.

"Hey, Wonder Boy, how'd it go?" Millicent asked.

"They served brussels sprouts," he said. "I wasn't ready for brussels sprouts."

"I'm sorry," said Aunt Emily. "I hate them too."

"I left when it was time to sing. We never had a plan for the birthday song. I didn't know what to do. But there were parts that were fun."

Millicent patted the stairs. Elvis sat down next to her.

"The tree frogs will be out soon," said Aunt Emily. "We haven't listened to them in a long time." She stroked Millicent's hair. "When you were a little girl, you wouldn't miss an evening of your tree frog symphony." She nudged Elvis. "You'll like this. They're only about an inch or two high, but these guys know how to give a concert."

A single frog went "quonk quonk quonk" in the shadows. From the other side of the yard, another one answered.

Millicent sighed. "When I was in my dorm room in college, I used to think about them. No matter what was happening in the city at night, I knew every evening this time of year, deep in the Pinelands, those frogs would be here in the trees. It's one of the best parts about this place."

Some more frogs joined in.

"Like my musical minute," said Elvis. "No matter what happens in the world or even to me, at 8:04 people are singing."

Aunt Emily smiled at him. "It's a great comfort."

There was a chorus of frogs now. They echoed off the trees.

"Millicent got her letter from the University of Hawaii today," Aunt Emily explained. "She didn't get the librarian position."

"They don't want me," Millicent said plainly.

"There are other libraries and other jobs," said Aunt Emily.

"Not in Hawaii. I was so close. It was between me and one other librarian," said Millicent. "I was so sure they'd pick me. I was so close to getting it."

The frogs faded. A new, higher-pitched call took their place.

"The cicadas are taking over now," announced Millicent, "and I am not a fan. I'm going inside."

Aunt Emily followed her. Elvis sat alone on the front porch. The spider was back. The web was thick, gauzy, and right smack in the middle of the posts of the front steps, exactly like it was before. A moth wriggled in the far corner. Before the spider reached its prey, Elvis moved into the back yard.

A sad sound rose above the cicada calls. It found its way between the din of the insects and the "whet whet" of the saw-whet owl.

It was a violin.

There was no mistake. This wasn't a frog or owl or creature of the night.

Someone was playing the violin. Or trying to. The notes were thin and squeaky.

Elvis leaned in and listened.

If this was the song Cecilia hoped to hear, she was going to be very disappointed.

Aaron's Abuelo

Cicadas.

Busy buzzy things.

Elvis hated them. Especially now when they stopped him from following that sound of the violin.

Elvis moved away from the woods and hurried out front to the road. The cicada calls were softer here, not by much but enough for Elvis to trail the notes.

He stepped past Cheryl McKenzie's blueberry stand and the Old Church. The Lost Treasures Thrift and Throwaway Store was lit up bright, like Mrs. Herbert was expecting company. Elvis pressed his face up against the window. There was no one around. He pushed the door, but it was locked up tight.

Mrs. Herbert must have left the lights on when she closed the place.

The violin player changed songs, squeaking out quick, fast notes. They were easier to follow.

Elvis made his way around the gravel path. The music grew louder. A dim light glowed behind Barnegat Al's Auto Repair.

Jacob Clayton sat outside on a bench, his violin tucked under his chin and the bow in his hand.

Elvis stood in the shadows and watched him play.

Violins are fussy instruments. They have no patience for beginners. When Jacob played, the violin complained with a screeching sound.

"No wonder you're having problems. You're not holding the bow right," Elvis blurted out. "You're changing directions too suddenly."

Jacob stopped.

Now the only sound was cicadas.

"What do you mean?" Jacob asked finally.

"You're going in every direction. Your bow has to flow. Point it one way."

Jacob tried again. This time, he kept the bow straight. He played a single clear note.

"Better." Elvis nodded.

"Hey, Aaron, I didn't know you played. Millicent never mentioned it."

"Well, I, no. I mean, not really. I know about the violin, because my, um, my grandfather plays." Elvis's grandparents had died early, the last one when he was three, and he never got to know any of them. But *Aaron* could have a grandfather. His friend Ramon had a grandfather who played the violin, a big bold man with candy in his pockets. They met on *TweenStar* family day. Ramon called him "abuelo." Once Elvis called him that too. He liked Ramon's abuelo. They even joked around about starting their own band someday.

"My abuelo," Elvis said out loud. "My abuelo plays."

"And you learned all this from watching?"

"He plays a lot. Family gatherings. Get-togethers. All the time."

"My dad played all the time too, and I never learned anything from just watching," said Jacob. He grabbed a cake of rosin and rubbed it on the bow.

Elvis took a deep breath. No wonder he liked standing under those old trees. The rosin had the same piney smell.

"You're putting too much on the bow. Your notes sound jagged if you use too much of the stuff."

"How do you know how much to use?" asked Jacob.

"Rosin makes your bow less slippery. If you have a slippery

bow, then your notes will fade. I made up this . . . I mean my *abuelo* created this rap."

"Your abuelo raps?"

"It goes like this. 'Rosin up the bow when your notes are low. Then the sound will grow.' "

"Did anyone ever tell you that you have a great voice?"

Elvis took two steps back. "How would you know? I only sang one line."

"Just the same. I know a good voice when I hear it. So all that stuff you learned from your abuelo and you never tried to play?" He held his violin out toward Elvis.

Elvis touched the strings. Then he handed it back.

"I'm a guitar player myself. That's my first instrument and it's a much easier one to learn," said Jacob. "I'd play music all the time if I didn't need money. That's why I work here at Barnegat Al's."

About ten thousand cicadas echoed his words.

"They never shut up, do they?" asked Elvis.

"The singing cicadas?"

"Singing? That's hardly singing."

Jacob laughed. "They're the loudest insects in the world, you know. It's the males that are making all the racket to impress the females." He leaned back on the bench. "I guess that happens in all species, humans too."

He took the violin and held it like a guitar, pretending to

strum on the strings. "Maybe Millicent would pay more attention to me if I were a famous musician."

"You mean like a superstar? I don't think she'd be impressed," Elvis said, grateful that for the first time since he got here, he could say something that he knew was true.

Another Superstar and the Price of Fame

In the Pinelands, the Jersey Devil is a superstar too. Like Elvis, he's had his share of bad publicity. When you're that famous, it doesn't take much. A small lapse in judgment. A single mistake.

There was that time one winter when he flew a little too close to a house by a river, and the man who lived there heard his webbed wings flutter. That tiny glimmer of recognition was all it took. That and a well-placed story in the morning paper. Suddenly there were thousands of Jersey Devil sightings. Newspapers were filled with articles. They closed schools. People refused to go to work. They called it a "phenomenal week."

And the things they said. They were so unkind. They

called his voice a "squawk and a whistle" and said he emitted a "curious glow." They accused him of "spurting flames," and, to be totally honest, he's never spurted a thing in his entire life.

The old-timers say the poor Devil took it all to heart. His tail grew three inches longer and his horns grew sharper. Those big batlike wings grew more webbed. He turned, well, more devilish, which is exactly what people expected him to be.

It's true, you know.

It was in all the papers.

The Philadelphia Record.

The Public Ledger.

Perhaps there was even an article about it in *Celebrity Scoop Magazine.*

A Slip and a Fall

Sometimes RJ was too chatty for his own good. When this happened Cecilia would walk very slowly in front of the Old Church. And for those brief moments, there'd be blessed silence. But it's a small town and a small church and you couldn't keep walking past it forever.

As soon as they reached the Wares Grove Hunt Club, he started again. "What makes you think Elvis Ruby will come with us anyway?"

"My mom called Aunt Emily. She said he would."

"He might have changed his mind," said RJ. "Did you see how he got last night at 'Happy Birthday'? What was with that headache?"

"What else was he supposed to do? You tried to trick him into singing. You shouldn't have done that."

"Well, you weren't nice to him either."

"What do you mean?"

"You served him brussels sprouts. Everyone knows that Elvis Ruby doesn't like brussels sprouts. His hatred is legendary. It was even mentioned on the *TweenStar* show once."

Cecilia shoved her hands into her pockets. "You've had my mother's brussels sprouts. They're really good. I thought he'd like them."

"I'm going to tell him I know who he is," RJ announced.

Cecilia glanced at the front porch of Piney Pete's, making sure Elvis hadn't come out yet before she answered. "If you tell him that you know, he'll never trust me again."

"How do you know he trusts you now? And maybe he shouldn't trust you since you did tell."

"You're the only one I told," she hissed. "And you told too. So maybe I shouldn't trust you either."

They were almost in front of the Pancake Palace. "I already told you," said RJ. "I only told my mom. I didn't know moms counted."

"Of course they count." Cecilia gave him a gentle poke. "Look," she said, "he wants to be called Aaron. And you should call someone what they want to be called."

"I want to be called the grand ultimate emperor of the state of New Jersey. But that doesn't make it so."

"Aaron," Cecilia said. "His name is Aaron."

"If I tell him I know, maybe he'll stop mumbling and look me in the eye."

"He's trying to hide his identity."

"But I *know* his identity."

"But he doesn't know you know."

When Elvis leaped down the steps of the Pancake Palace, RJ drew out his name long and hard. "Hello, Aaarrrrroooonn."

"Hi," said Elvis, but his skyward gaze gave RJ plenty of time to make I-told-you-so faces at Cecilia.

Cecilia pushed RJ. "Let's go."

"Wait!?"

They turned around.

Elizabeth stood behind them, wearing shimmery lip gloss and a flowered shirt. "I'm coming with you." And her eyelashes fluttered.

RJ glanced down at her feet. "In those shoes?"

She was wearing ones with tiny heels.

Elizabeth gave her brother something much more than a playful push. "Of course. Let's go."

RJ kicked at the sand and shuffled as he walked, all the while keeping a sharp eye on his older sister. It was disgusting really. All that attention she gave Elvis for doing nothing. Elvis cleared his throat, and Elizabeth practically applauded. Elvis asked, "How much farther?" and Elizabeth answered with encouraging smiles. RJ had been her brother for eleven years now and he never remembered this much warmth and compassion. It was a side of Elizabeth he hadn't seen before. Frankly, he hoped he'd never have to see it again.

They traveled in single file. Cecilia was first. Then Elvis, with Elizabeth trailing so close that she sometimes accidentally stepped on the heels of his shoes. Then finally RJ.

They were deep into the pygmy forest when Cecilia stopped at a fork in the path. She stood with her mouth open, facing the direction of the wind.

"Catching flies?" asked Elvis. And Elizabeth, with her fluttering eyes, giggled.

"Nope. I'm tasting spring," Cecilia said. "My dad says this is the only place in the world where you can taste the seasons. It's the sugar sand. When the wind sweeps it up, it mixes with the pollen from the trees."

"Cecilia does stuff like this all the time," explained RJ, and he said it in a friendly guy-to-guy way, straight to Elvis Ruby. But RJ might as well have been talking to the pines. Elvis never even glanced in his direction.

RJ kicked up more sugar sand, secretly hoping he got some of it in Elvis's shoes and, with a little luck, in Elizabeth's too. When neither one noticed, RJ stood shoulder to shoulder next to Cecilia and opened his mouth wide.

"Whatever," said Elizabeth. But as soon as she saw Elvis try it, Elizabeth was beside him, standing against the wind, her mouth gaping open like a hungry bird.

"I can taste the wild orchids and the pink curly ferns and the cranberry bogs and the sphagnum moss and the cedar swamps," Cecilia said. "Oh oh oh, and I can taste wild blueberries too."

"Pitch pines," said RJ. "All I get is the taste of pitch pines."

"Yeah. Me too. Pitch pines," said Elizabeth. She nodded encouragingly at Elvis.

Cecilia was doing that jumping around thing again. "Can you feel it? Can you taste the Pinelands?"

Elvis held his mouth open. "Not really. I taste something bitter maybe," said Elvis, and RJ thought his tone was whiny.

They were walking in a different place now. Instead of the pygmy forest filled with stubby pines, larger trees pushed their way to the sky, blocking out the sunlight.

It was RJ who brought up the Jersey Devil. It was bound to happen. Seriously, you can't take two steps into the Pinelands without someone bringing him up. "You know about him, right?" he asked.

"He's on the place mats at the Pancake Palace," said Elvis.

"They say he's here too. In the woods around us." RJ made loud, scary ghost noises and circled around Elvis. His last "wooowoooo" was right in Elvis's face.

Elizabeth grabbed RJ's shirt and pulled him back.

"So, Aaron." RJ said the name slow and loud, with eye rolls at Cecilia. "Do you believe in him?"

Elvis shrugged. "I don't know. There are a lot of creatures that people think they've seen. Every place has one. The Loch Ness monster. Big Foot. And you can't go into a theater or stadium without someone saying they saw a ghost."

RJ glanced at Elizabeth and Cecilia. From the looks on their faces, he thought they heard it too. Elvis had slipped. It was a mistake for him to mention theaters. Only someone who spent a lot of time backstage would know about the ghost stories. If RJ didn't know his secret already, Elvis might have blown his cover.

RJ wanted to tell him that too. He wanted to warn him that he needed to be more careful. But when he saw the glare Cecilia gave him through her giant glasses, he kept quiet.

Elvis appeared to be unaware of his blunder. While they walked, he talked some more. "I don't know about this place." He waved his hand at the Pinelands and grinned at Cecilia. "There seem to be a lot of things hiding out in these woods."

RJ watched how Cecilia grinned back.

"My friend Ashley's older brother said he heard something

in the woods when he was camping." Elizabeth was falling behind, the heels of her shoes sinking deep into the ground.

Elvis turned and waited for her.

"Cecilia believes in the Jersey Devil," said RJ. "Don't you, Ceily?"

Cecilia hesitated.

"That he grew bat wings and a tail and flew out the window?" RJ egged her on.

"He was unwanted," Cecilia said, softly. "Who knows what an unwanted child would do?"

They reached a spot where the trees grew straight and tall and blocked out the sunlight. The bark twisted around each trunk like the stripes in a peppermint candy cane.

"What is this place?" Elvis asked.

"It's the cedar swamp," said RJ.

And even though his answer was extremely helpful, Elvis didn't even give him as much as a nod. A friendly nod would have been nice.

"We're getting closer to where I was born," said Cecilia.

Their steps slowed. Moss grew in hummocks beneath them, jutting up in jagged mounds. Tiny flowers sprouted from the hollows.

"Here it is," said Cecilia. "We're almost there." She pointed to a shallow stream.

The water had a reddish glow.

Elvis looked up at the trees and at the way the sunlight hardly made it to the ground. RJ could tell that he was searching for a reason.

"It's not a trick," RJ explained. "It's stained red." He watched Elvis reach down into the stream and cup the water into his hands.

"How can this be?" Elvis asked.

RJ leaned alongside him and gave an evil laugh. "It's not really water. It's the blood of the Jersey Devil."

Elvis backed away from the stream so fast that he tripped over a hummock.

"No, it's not," shouted Cecilia and Elizabeth at the exact same time.

"It's called cedar water," said Elizabeth. "It's supposed to be that color." She gave RJ a sharp rap on the head.

Cecilia pointed to the trees. "Something in the roots turns it that color. And the soil has iron, like rust. It's part of nature. It's how things are here."

The girls helped Elvis up, clucking and fussing around him like he was a baby chick.

"Sorry about that. I was joking around," said RJ, all the time trying to hide his gloats from Elizabeth, who would certainly give him another rap on the head if she noticed.

"Good one," said Elvis. "You had me fooled." For the first time ever, Elvis Ruby looked RJ straight in the eye.

And that was all that RJ had wanted.

The Secret Is Spilled . . . Again

While Elvis and the others stood near the red-stained waters, Mrs. Herbert sat at her favorite table at Piney Pete's. She heaved sighs, heavy ones that took the cheeriness out of the entire room.

Aunt Emily glanced to make sure no other customers were around. Then she sat down at the table and poured two cups of tea.

"Do you know what old books smell like?" Mrs. Herbert asked.

This time it was Aunt Emily's turn to sigh.

Another quiz.

It seemed that no matter how many years Mrs. Herbert

was retired, she could never forget that she had once been Aunt Emily's fifth-grade teacher.

She was always throwing questions at her. Yesterday she asked Aunt Emily why the moon glowed orange, and the day before she asked her if she knew what type of cranberries bounced. The cranberry question hurt. After all, Aunt Emily was a chef. She owned a restaurant in the Pinelands, a place known for its cranberries. *Of course* she knew that only the ripe ones bounced. But instead of saying that, she nodded politely while Mrs. Herbert explained all about them.

"Old books?" Aunt Emily put another spoonful of sugar in her tea. "I don't know. Mold, maybe?"

Mrs. Herbert smiled. "Obviously you've been sniffing the wrong books. When fine old books get even older, they smell exactly like vanilla. That's why the used book section is the nicest part of my store." She held her tea so the steam swirled around her. "Remember how my husband used to sniff the old yellowed pages? Those are the ones with the strongest scent."

"Of course I remember. How could I forget how much Mr. Herbert loved his books?" Aunt Emily patted Mrs. Herbert's hand. "So that's why the Lost Treasures Thrift and Throw-away Store always smells so sweet."

"Yep. It's a store secret." Mrs. Herbert nodded.

The two women sipped their tea.

"So now you know," said Mrs. Herbert. She closed her eyes and slurped.

And Aunt Emily had the feeling that it was her turn to share. "I have a secret too," she said.

"Is it about your pancakes?"

No, not that one. Never that one. "It's about Aaron," she said.

Mrs. Herbert looked around. "Where is he?"

"He, Cecilia, and RJ are off in the woods. I think Cecilia's taken a liking to him."

Mrs. Herbert nodded.

"You must promise not to tell, but there is something very special about him."

Mrs. Herbert brightened. "Tell me."

Yes, thought Aunt Emily. This is the right thing to do. Mrs. Herbert was going through such a difficult time now that Mr. Herbert was gone. And she helped take care of Millicent during the year of the divorce. And all those years ago, she'd been a very good fifth-grade teacher.

Besides, Aunt Emily couldn't resist. She couldn't handle any more of Mrs. Herbert's deep, sad sighs. She had to give her something that would cheer her up.

So Aunt Emily told.

"I knew there was something different about that boy."

Mrs. Herbert smacked her lips, tasting the sweetness of the secret, which was even more delicious than Aunt Emily's famous Piney Pete's Blues—and those were her favorites.

She thought of Sophia, her six-year-old granddaughter. Sophia lived in Florida, which was so far away, but her parents sent videos. There was one of Sophia dancing and singing the *TweenStar* theme song, and then ending with the words "I love you, Elvis Ruby."

And for a moment, a brief moment, the tiniest, briefest moment, Mrs. Herbert thought about calling her. And telling her.

It would be their secret. Something only a grandmother and granddaughter shared. She imagined Sophia's parents, her serious daughter, Claire, and her stodgy husband, Matthew, wearing their funny I-don't-know-what's-going-on looks while she and Sophia giggled on the phone. It would be something her granddaughter would remember all her life.

After all, Sophia was so far away. What harm would it do?

"You have to keep this a secret." Aunt Emily was almost begging now.

"Of course. Of course." But before Mrs. Herbert pushed thoughts of her granddaughter away, she imagined her doing that fancy step in the Elvis Ruby dance one last time. And she gave another one of her famous sighs. "Does Elvis play his instruments or sing anymore? He performed so beautifully on the show."

"Not since he got here," said Aunt Emily.

"I saw him on television. I watched it happen. That poor boy. He must have been under so much pressure."

"He doesn't talk about it."

Mrs. Herbert waved her hand around the Pancake Palace. "This place will do him good. And you will do him some good too."

Thirteen

If you want to keep track, the number is thirteen. That's how many people know.

Cecilia found out because she was wandering outside the night when Elvis stood under the pine trees and said his name.

And she told RJ.

Then RJ told his mom (and yes, moms count).

Elizabeth was a total accident. She happened to be sitting in the living room when they were talking and overheard bits and pieces. It's remarkable, really, since normally she's so glued to her cell phone that she never pays attention to anything her little brother says, even when he's standing two feet away from her shouting "time for dinner." But somehow the name "Elvis Ruby" found its way into her ears. She even stopped texting (which is something she never does). As soon as RJ left the room, Elizabeth raced into the kitchen demanding to be filled in. So RJ's mom is in the free and clear. It's not like she said anything. She only confirmed what her daughter already knew.

Elizabeth told her best friend, Ashley. She had to. How else could she explain why she stopped texting in the middle of a message? Besides, isn't that what best friends do?

And then she couldn't tell her one best friend without telling her other best friend, who also happens to be named Ashley. It was only right, and there would be huge problems if the second Ashley found out. Elizabeth swore them both to secrecy, if that makes any difference.

Of course Elvis knows. And his dad. And Cher.

And Aunt Emily. And Millicent.

And now, Mrs. Herbert knows.

So that makes . . . twelve.

The other person who knows is Amanda, a friend of Cher's. She plays the role of Brigitta in the traveling performance of the show *The Sound of Music*, the same one that Cher is performing in. Cher and Amanda are the two youngest children in the show and they spend tons of hours backstage together.

One night while a dozen singing nuns stood onstage belting out the song "How Do You Solve a Problem Like Maria?" Cher sat in the corner behind the curtains and told Amanda everything.

Here's an interesting fact about Amanda. She was the first contestant to get booted off *TweenStar* the same season that Elvis was on the show. Small world, right?

When you think about it, thirteen isn't really a lot, considering millions of people want to know the whereabouts of Elvis Ruby. So he should be okay, right? But it's no secret about secrets. They have a way of spreading like wildfire.

In the Pinelands, they know all about wildfire. Water seeps through the sandy soil and the land is always dry. It doesn't take much to start things. A tiny spark.

Don't worry. The trees are used to it. Those pitch pines that grow practically everywhere hold their pinecones for years, waiting for the fire. As soon as they feel the heat, they pop open and their seeds fall to the ground. And everything starts anew. They need the wildfires. They thrive in the heat.

Even the people have learned to adjust. They don't exactly thrive in a fire—that's not something humans do—but when you live in the Pinelands, you begin to think of the burning woods as part of life.

But we weren't really talking about wildfires. We were talking about secrets.

Wandering Bill

"Hey, Elvis, wake up."

He buried himself deeper in the blankets. The voices called him Elvis. He was having another dream.

"Elvis."

He opened his eyes. Dad and Cher stood over his bed. He reached out and grabbed them both.

"We thought we'd sneak in a visit," said his dad, still holding him tight.

"Did anyone see you?" Elvis looked out the window. "Were you followed? Those photographers would do that."

"Tell me about it," said Cher. "Now they're even starting to follow *me* around."

"This is going to blow over soon. They'll move on to

someone else. And it will all go away once you come back. They're all waiting for you to come back." Out of habit, his father closed the curtains and pulled Elvis away from the window.

"New haircut?" Elvis asked. Cher's hair was choppy, in a good way. It fell on her shoulders.

Cher nodded. "Guess what? I got a standing ovation the last seven shows. They loved me. Did you see my reviews?"

"They love her everywhere." Dad grabbed Cher and twirled her around. "The moment she walks onstage, you can almost feel the audience watching her. She steals every scene she's in. She's got that same quality that you have, Elvis."

"Oh," he said softly, and he hugged his sister tight.

A few minutes later, Aunt Emily and Millicent whipped up some late-night pancakes. Elvis stirred the batter. It was becoming his usual job. He was part of the Piney Pete's pancake-making team. And when he stirred, the pancakes were almost as good as Aunt Emily's.

He showed Cher how to wet her hand in the water and flick it onto the hot griddle. "When things get too hot, the water starts to bounce around. It's the Leidenfrost effect," he explained, which made Millicent smile.

When they sat down at the table, his father announced that they were the best pancakes ever. "Still using your grandfather's secret recipe?" he asked.

Aunt Emily nodded.

"Nothing ever changes here," Dad said.

"That's for sure," chimed in Millicent.

"And that's not a bad thing," Aunt Emily said. There was something vinegary in her voice.

"There's a secret ingredient," Elvis whispered to Cher. "That's what makes it special." But he stopped when Aunt Emily put her finger to her lips.

As soon as they were done eating, Millicent and Aunt Emily went back to bed. Cher dozed off on the living room couch.

Elvis and his dad stood outside on the front porch watching that crazy spider weave its web.

"I've never seen one this big," said his dad. It was so thick and gauzy that even the moonlight was having a hard time finding its way through.

They stepped down the stairs. Dad stared at the sign that said "Caution. Spider Busy Spinning." Millicent had painted it. "Is this really the best thing for business?"

"The tourists seem to like him. Sometimes they ask to eat

out here so they can watch him work." Come to think of it, even three-year-old Jack Junior left the web alone, and that was something.

Elvis followed his father as he walked around the Palace and into the back yard. They sat on the old bench.

"Did you know that some of those pine trees have names?"

"I know. Emily and I named them when we were kids." Dad pointed to the trees. "Those four, right? I forgot the name of that one."

"The one that bulges out? That's the Pregnant Lady, and the one that's leaning all the way over—"

His dad interrupted. "I know that one. Emily named it for me. Before I took the stage name 'Austin.' Back when I was William Ruber."

"You're Bill? You're the tree, Bill?"

Dad nodded. "The one that looks like it's trying to escape. That's me, Wandering Bill. I couldn't wait to leave this place. Nothing but pine trees and sand. Made me feel closed in. Give me a big city any day."

Elvis reached down to the ground and picked up a twig. "I like it here."

His father pointed to the back, this time to the hundreds of trees that yawned into the darkness. "Look at them. They're all the same. Same size and none of them are very tall. Same stubby trees. Same twisty branches. They say there's no reason why they're short like that. Scientists say they're the same types of trees as the ones that grow tall out west. They just don't want to grow tall. Why they don't want to stand up and be noticed is something I don't understand."

Elvis wasn't sure what to say. Normally when he and his dad talked, it was about music and chord changes and performing onstage. This was his first parental lecture. He didn't know where to look either. Finally he settled on watching the spider.

"Do you want to talk about what happened?"

Elvis shook his head. "No."

"You're not the first to freeze onstage, you know. It happens to musicians and singers all the time. There's a doctor in New York City . . ."

"I don't need a doctor. I'm fine."

"No, you're not. Music is such a big part of you. You were playing before you could walk, Elvis. I should never have let you go on that show."

"I wanted to go on it."

"Yeah, but you also want ice cream every night for dinner. I should have said no." His dad mussed up his hair, like he had a hundred times before. But this time, it was sandy-colored and short, dry from the hair dye and the sun. "It's not easy being the father of someone like you. You have such talent. It would be wrong if I didn't push you to use it. And when I pushed too hard, that was wrong too."

In the distance, a violin played. Jacob's song matched the conversation perfectly. Sad. Sweet. Wistful. Elvis had to smile.

When Jacob played a squeaky note, his dad looked down at his watch. "We'd better go. We have a long drive to Wilmington. Once this tour is over, you'll come back to New York. We'll stay there awhile. You'll see that doctor. It will be better, Elvis."

Elvis looked out at the pine tree Bill and then straight at his father, the former Bill now known as Austin. "I'd prefer it if you called me Aaron."

But There Is Music in the Pines

"Hey," said Jacob, "if it isn't the nieto of the violin player."

"Nieto?" asked Elvis.

"That's grandson in Spanish. I thought someone who has an abuelo would know that."

"Right." Elvis sat down on the bench next to Jacob and slapped at a mosquito.

"I was hoping you'd stop by, but it got so late that I thought you weren't coming."

"We had some company. It was hard to get away."

"Was it your abuelo? I should like to meet him someday. Maybe we could play together." Jacob played a few quick notes. "But not until I get a little bit better on this thing."

"That could take a while," said Elvis.

Jacob played a slow tune. "How am I doing?"

His bow slipped, his finger placement was off, and his instrument was pointed in the wrong direction.

"Better," said Elvis. "What song are you playing, anyway?"

"It's an old love song. I'm trying to learn it to play for Millicent. She will have to fall in love with me then." Jacob jabbed him with his bow. "Don't tell, okay? It's going to be a surprise."

Elvis nodded.

The violin whined.

"Maybe you should play your guitar, instead," Elvis suggested.

"I thought that a violin would be a better instrument for a love song."

Elvis thought about it. "A guitar would work." But then again so would a flute. A horn. A banjo. A tambourine. A trombone. The drums. When you're mixing music and love, there really is no bad combination.

"So does your abuelo have any more pointers?" asked Jacob. Together they worked on the song. After a while, it began to sound . . . well . . . like an actual song.

Elvis slapped at another mosquito. "Why do you always play outside anyway?"

"There's something about being outside in nature. It's healing. It's freeing. And have you ever seen anything more beautiful in your life?" He pointed to the trees that Elvis's father had called stubby.

"Yeah, right. And let me guess, you've heard music in the pines," said Elvis. Another mosquito landed on him. He took a slow aim and then slapped down fast.

Jacob waved his bow like it was a sword. "But there *is* music in the pines. I know exactly where it is. I can show you. We'll go the day after tomorrow. This Saturday night. You ask Cecilia and I'll ask Millicent and I'll take you to it."

"How do you know about Cecilia?"

Jacob played the song all the way through before he answered.

"That you and Cecilia have been seen together? It's a small town. People gossip. Everyone knows everything here."

Albert Music Hall

On Saturday night, the car pulled into the parking lot of the Frederic A. Priff Elementary School. "You wanted music in the Pinelands? Well, here it is," said Jacob.

Cecilia sank into the back seat. "I thought we were going into the woods to listen for a song."

"I didn't know we were going here," said Millicent. "You told me we were going for pie." She turned to the back seat and looked square at Elvis. "Be careful," she mouthed.

"I thought I'd surprise you all," said Jacob. "We are going for pie. It's delicious here. And there's music here too and we're still in the Pinelands, so everyone should be happy."

"At the school?" asked Elvis.

Jacob laughed. "Nope. The building next to it. Albert Music Hall."

The words "music hall" made Elvis think of sparkling chandeliers and giant stages and stage lights from every angle. The *TweenStar* music hall was a glittery, sparkly place. And his dad played in some of them when they traveled on his world tours. There was one in Austria that looked like a castle.

This was a Doc Bashful of a building if there ever was one. If you didn't know it was here, you'd pass by it twice, three times if you were unlucky. Nothing about the outside shone.

"Not what you were expecting, was it?" said Jacob. "This place is famous around here though. It's named for two brothers, George and Joe Albert, who started playing music deep in the woods. In the summer evenings, even the deer wandered by to listen. Eventually it got so crowded they had to find a bigger place. And when that place burned down, they moved here." He opened the car door. "Come on, let's go."

Jacob hurried toward the music hall. Millicent, Cecilia, and Elvis dragged behind.

The lobby was lined with posters, newspaper clippings, and photos. The entire hall smelled of sauerkraut and apple pie.

"The music here is great. And so is the food," said Jacob. He put his arm around Millicent. "They have picnic tables in the back of the auditorium so you can eat and still watch the musicians perform." He pointed to a table. "Look, that's what the Blades are doing."

At one of the crowded tables, Jack Junior poured drops of milk on his mother's plate, then slurped it with a straw. Andrea and Big Jack were so busy listening to the band play onstage that they didn't seem to notice. Elvis made a mental note never to play banjo music if he wanted to get rid of the Blades.

Millicent pushed them all in the opposite direction. "Come on, this way."

Live music. It was the first time he'd heard it since that day on *TweenStar*. Like gravity, it pulled at him. Elvis stepped toward the stage.

Millicent pulled him back. "Where are you going?"

Somewhere in the crowd a voice shouted, "Elvis Ruby!" And Elvis slunk behind Cecilia and waited.

"Did you hear that?" he asked.

"The boy over there with the curly hair," she whispered. "He's the one who said your name."

But the boy didn't even look Elvis's way. Instead he rubbed his long curly hair. It flopped in his eyes when he nodded to his friend.

"It's the latest hairstyle, Wonder Boy," said Millicent. "It's called the Ruby cut. All the boys your age have it." Then she grinned. "I bet you'd look good in it."

They hadn't been seated for three minutes when Cecilia gave Elvis a nudge. "Come on. Let's go."

The song the band was performing onstage made Elvis tap his feet. He pretended not to notice Cecilia until she poked at him again.

"Please," she whispered. "There's a gift shop and there's pie."

"But there's music," he hissed, and he tapped his feet some more.

"It's not for me," she said. She pulled at him until he followed.

They waved to the Blades as they passed by the picnic tables and headed back to the lobby.

"You kids see anything you like?" the lady behind the souvenir counter asked. "T-shirts are on sale today. There's a bunch of them on the rack. You can head into the back and take a look."

Cecilia scooted under the counter.

"She's gonna be a while. There are a lot to go through," the lady said to Elvis. "You can either go back there with her or you can head to the Pickin' Shed." She leaned over the counter.

"Don't tell anyone I told you this, but some of the best music of the night isn't always found on the stage. You can find it in the Pickin' Shed. It's where musicians go to jam. Anyone can join in. Old, young, beginners, old-timers." She straightened up some postcards and laughed. "Even you can play, if you want to."

Elvis called over to Cecilia, "Be right back," and was out the door before she could answer.

The Pickin' Shed was a small room, more crowded than the auditorium. In the center of it, a man with a beard played some chords on a guitar. He nodded to a woman with short hair and pointy glasses who strummed a banjo. Next to them, a man played a violin.

Elvis found a place to stand near the wall and closed his eyes to listen to the song. It was one he'd never heard before.

"Hey, son. Do you play?"

He opened his eyes, surprised to see the fiddler standing in front of him, holding out the violin and bow. All eyes were on him.

"How'd you know?" he asked, too surprised to deny it.

"The way you were moving your hands. It was as if you were playing along." The violin was between them. "I can show you this song," the man added. He slowed down the tune, and played it in small bits. But Elvis didn't need to hear it again. It was already inside him.

Elvis reached for the violin, then pulled back. What if someone recognized him? Millicent had remarked the other day that his hair was growing in. "You have roots!" she told him. "The new growth in your hair is a different color from the dyed part. And it's getting longer. We have to fix that or you'll start to look like Elvis Ruby."

The man offered him the bow. For the second time, he pulled his hand back. "Don't be shy," said the fiddler.

His father could name a musician by hearing him play. Even if he'd never heard the song before, he knew who was making the music. "The way you play is as personal as a fingerprint," his father said. "All the great musicians have their own style."

Elvis wondered what would happen if he played. Would people hear his notes and say, "That's the *TweenStar* kid. That's Elvis Ruby"?

There were ten thousand good reasons not to play, but it didn't matter. It was as if the strings from the violin curled themselves around him and wrangled out a single word.

Yes.

The Pickin' Shed

The room grew quiet. Elvis played the fiddler's song. The woman who played the banjo began to sing. And the guitar player gave a low whistle and whispered, "That kid knows what he's doing." He strummed with him.

There were words to this song. Something about still waters, pine smoke, and forgotten towns. But Elvis didn't need the words to know what the song was about. For the first time, he heard the beat of this place. Not the "let me out, let me out" beat that his father felt. This was what the Pinelands felt like to Cecilia, Jacob Clayton, Aunt Emily, and everyone else who loved it.

The door banged open, and Cecilia walked in. Elvis missed a note.

A boy with the Ruby haircut whispered something to his mom. They both pointed at Elvis, and they left in a hurry.

He missed a second note.

A woman in a flowered shirt stretched and yawned.

The violin squeaked.

Someone laughed.

The song faded, like the car engine the night his father and Cher drove away. Soon it disappeared completely. Wrong notes came out. The short-haired woman with the banjo winced. The guitar player stopped playing.

Elvis stood in the center of the room, the violin at his side.

The man who gave him the fiddle leaned over and pointed toward Cecilia. "Pretty girls will do that to you. They'll make you forget everything, even your music."

Was Cecilia pretty? He'd never noticed before.

The man on the guitar grinned. "Yep, you're not the first guy here to lose your beat because of a girl, that's for sure."

But it wasn't Cecilia. He felt the same way he had that night he froze on *TweenStar*. He was in the place where the music faded.

"Let's hear it for . . . what did you say your name was?" asked the banjo player.

"Aaron," he said, but the sound of his own voice felt distant.

"Let's hear it for Aaron," she said to the crowd.

There were halfhearted cheers and some applause. He was out the door before it ended.

Cecilia was speaking. She was standing right next to him, and Elvis could see her mouth move, but she seemed so far away it was hard to hear.

"Are you okay?" Finally Cecilia's words broke through the rushing sound in his head. "Do you want me to get Millicent?"

They stood outside the Pickin' Shed. Elvis put his ear up against the wall. "Are they playing an Elvis Presley song?"

"I don't care what they're playing," said Cecilia. "I asked you if you wanted me to get Millicent. Are you okay?"

Someone opened the door. A few bars of the song escaped before the door closed again. "You know what song that is, don't you?"

Cecilia crossed her arms in front of her. "No. I'm sorry. I don't."

"It's 'Heartbreak Hotel.'" Now the rushing sound gave way to panic.

"So?"

"It's an Elvis Presley song."

"So?" Cecilia shrugged.

"That was my song. The one I was supposed to sing the night I froze." Elvis paced back and forth. "They know. They're playing Elvis Presley because of me," he said.

Cecilia put her hands on her hips. "Maybe it has nothing to do with you. Maybe they're playing Elvis Presley because they like Elvis Presley."

Elvis paced along the back of the shed. "What are they playing now?"

Cecilia pressed her head up to listen. "I can't tell," she whispered. "I can never tell."

"You know it's easier to hear from the inside," a deep voice said, laughing. "You're allowed to stay inside and listen."

The man who played the fiddle stood by the wall. "Why don't you come back and give it another try? What did you say your name was again?"

"Aaron." He gulped out the name and ran his hand over his hair. Was it over? Did the man know who he really was?

"Aaron," the man repeated. "Hope to see you again." He held out the fiddle. "Here. It's filled with scrapes and nicks. But I've got a bunch more. I find the broken ones and I fix them. How about you take this and practice."

Elvis opened his mouth to say no, but Cecilia grabbed it. "Thank you. He'd love to." She started to do that jump-up-and-down thing she did whenever she got excited, but they were tiny jumps. Elvis could tell she was doing her best to hold it all in.

"You were almost magical in there," said the man. "It was as if the Pinelands itself found its way inside you."

"I knew it." Cecilia pointed to Elvis, and her jumps grew to leaps and bounds. "I knew you had it in you. I knew you'd be magical." She turned to the man. "I knew he'd be magical."

He put his hands up for her to calm down. "But I stopped," said Elvis. "Right in the middle of the song. There's no magic when you stop in the middle."

"Yeah," said the man. "That happens sometimes when you get distracted by the crowd. It's nothing to worry about. Everyone plays the wrong notes now and then."

The song in the Pickin' Shed changed and the man left. Elvis could hear the music go louder and then get muffled again as the door opened and closed.

For a long time Elvis stood with his ear pressed against the wall, listening to the dim sounds of singing and laughter.

What the Fiddler Knew

If there was a song, if there really was a Pinelands song, where would it hide? On a sandy path? In the needles of the pines? Perhaps in the leaves of the humped bladderwort, a rare and delicate yellow flower that lives on the banks of the cedar swamp stream. If an unsuspecting tadpole swims too close, then *Snap*. The leaves close tight, the tadpole is trapped, and the lovely carnivorous humped bladderwort enjoys a tasty meal. A deadly place for a tadpole. Yes. But perhaps a perfect spot to hide a song.

In the old days, the fiddler named Sammy Buck bragged he heard it all the time. "It's like a tune that's in the air," he told all his friends. He went into the woods with his fiddle to listen to it every chance he got. He was the type of guy who laughed a lot and wasn't afraid of much, so the day he saw the Jersey Devil searching in the salt bog by the tall grass, he called him over for a talk. "All these years and you've never heard the music once?" he asked. The Jersey Devil bowed his head in shame.

After that they had one or two polite conversations and Sammy offered to help the Devil look for the song. "Not sure why you're having such a hard time. Every time I go into the woods, it's there."

But then someone found out about Sammy talking to the Devil, and they told someone else who told someone else who told someone else . . . Well, you know how things start. And everyone agreed that it wasn't right for Sammy to help such a creature.

They called the Jersey Devil "hideous." And they used words like "brutal" and "gruesome." And the Devil took all their words very seriously. His tail grew a few more inches and his teeth grew sharper. And that wingspan got to be what it is today. He became everything they said he was and everything they thought a Jersey Devil should be. When Sammy Buck saw how their words made the Devil change, he shook his head sadly. "Poor Devil," he said. "Now I know why you've never found the music. You can search the Pinelands far and wide for the next hundred and fifty years and you never will."

To hide his tears, the Devil stared out at the trees. Before Sammy Buck had a chance to tell him more, the Devil flew away.

A Dedication

Elvis was quiet on the car ride home. Cecilia sat in the back seat alongside him, hiding the violin under her jacket.

Millicent turned up the volume of the radio and hummed along. It was a slow soulful tune.

While the car turned around one bend and then another, Elvis stared out the window, tapping his fingers in time with the beat.

The song ended. The DJ spoke. "Here's the new one by this year's winner of *TweenStar.*"

Millicent reached over to change the station.

"No, wait," said Elvis.

In the rearview mirror he saw Millicent stare.

"Really, let's listen."

When Millicent took her hand off the dial, Jasmeen's voice poured out of the radio. It seemed so real that it made him shiver. There was a short interview. She talked about winning and what it felt like when they crowned her the new *Tween-Star*. And that made him shiver too.

He liked Jasmeen. That night that everything happened, he was sitting backstage, and Jasmeen sat down beside him. She and Ramon were the only two contestants who went anywhere near him. The others brushed by him fast, like they were worried that what he had done was contagious.

After it all happened, Jasmeen put her hand on his shoulder. "It could have happened to any of us. You just never know." She even offered to dedicate a song to him. Jasmeen was famous for her heartfelt dedications.

He knew she'd won. Even though he stayed off the Internet, avoided papers and magazines, people talked. He heard the customers at the Pancake Palace. He saw coming attractions for shows when he watched television with Aunt Emily. It was too big a story for it not to trickle out even to the person who never wanted to know.

Jasmeen's voice piped into the car. "I'd like to dedicate this next song to Elvis Ruby and to all the others with shattered dreams."

There it was, his dedication, just like she promised.

She sang the *TweenStar* Goodbye Song.

It never goes the way you plan.
The stars have their own designs.
Still, you're gonna shine.
You'll find a way.

This was his song. He'd made it famous serenading all those losing contestants with his violin.

Sometimes you have to lose to win.
You think you've reached the end.

Jasmeen was singing his song.

Forget about what never was.
Find a way to begin again.

He put his hands over his ears, but he could still hear the last line.

And in the darkest night, reach for the moon.

Revealed in a Whisper

They turned the song into a mashup, a crazy mix of lyrics and catchy quotes from the *TweenStar* contestants. Jasmeen's "To Elvis Ruby and to all the others with shattered dreams" repeated throughout the song. Elvis's own words from an interview he hardly remembered were put in after the refrain. "Music is my life. Playing and singing is what I was meant to do." His words were soft and stretchy in the background.

If it was someone else's song, he'd have loved the way it was mashed together. He would have loved the haunting sound of the violin and the graceful notes from the guitar. Was that him playing? It would have been easy to add it in from one of the *TweenStar* shows. Was that guitar playing Ramon's?

This song should have been his. It should have been his voice pouring out of the radio. He should be the one on Broadway. And in the recording studios. And it should have been him living in the *TweenStar* mansion.

And so he hated every note.

But he was the only one in the world who seemed to hate it.

By the next morning, it was all over the place. On television. The radio. The video went viral on the Internet. But worse was how it snuck into Piney Pete's Pancake Palace. The song got served up with the pancakes.

"Hey, kid, do you have that new song?" the two kayakers from up north asked, and he was surprised because they didn't seem the type to like this one. It was his first request.

Elvis was filling up the sugar bowls when he caught Aunt Emily singing to herself.

"What are you doing? How can you hum it?" he asked.

"The song got inside me," she confessed. "It happens with music. There was nothing I could do to shake it out of my system. I had to sing it away."

After that every time they passed each other, she whispered to him, "I'm sorry."

Finally he whispered, "Me too."

He reached for empty plates on the table. They were sticky. Empty plates here were always sticky. He was growing tired of sticky.

And he wasn't sure he ever again wanted to pour another cup of coffee.

Aunt Emily took him aside. "Somehow this will work out. Things always happen for the best."

Millicent, holding a plate of Reds, overheard them. "The best? Are you kidding me?" Then she grabbed Elvis's arm and pulled him toward her. "Don't you let people tell you that. Ever. Jasmeen has a song on the radio and you're stuck here. You have every right to feel rotten about what happened to you."

Aunt Emily placed her hand on his shoulder. "Millicent is wrong. There has to be a good reason why you didn't win," she said. "Because how can you go on if you don't believe that?" She waved her plate of Piney Pete's Blues.

Elvis stood, sandwiched between them. The pancakes steamed.

"Jasmeen is taking bows on Broadway, living in a mansion with a petting zoo, and getting her nails done with Miley Cyrus, and this poor kid's stuck in New Jersey cleaning up pancake crumbs. How is that for the best?" Millicent said in a loud angry whisper. "Sometimes things happen and it's not for the best."

All three of them began talking in hissing whispers, forgetting themselves, forgetting where they were and why they should be quiet.

Nothing gets more attention than a loud angry whisper. Every customer in the restaurant turned to listen.

Some of them at least had the good sense to pretend they weren't. The two women in the corner poured syrup on their pancakes, only half glancing their way. Mrs. Herbert wrapped the string around her tea bag and drained it into the cup.

The two kayakers were much more obvious. Their chairs scraped on the floor as they turned them for a better view.

"No libraries and luaus for me. No singing onstage for Elvis. How is this good? For either one of us."

That's when they looked around and realized that people were listening. Aunt Emily turned back to the customers. "Free pancakes, anyone?"

The two kayakers hurried out. This time they left a fifty.

Waiting for the Sparks

Here's something else about wildfires in the Pinelands. The old-timers can tell when things are going to burn. It's not magic, really. All they have to do is look around. The air turns dry. The ground is covered with pine needles. The winds grow strong. When things turn like that, they know it's coming. So the old-timers watch. And they get ready.

And they wait. It's never easy waiting for a wildfire. That kind of tension is hard to take.

It's the same thing after you've spilled a secret. It's the powerlessness that you feel, knowing that something is going to happen but not being able to do anything about it, that will make you crazy.

But we weren't talking about secrets. We were talking about wildfires.

Or were we?

The next morning, Elizabeth sat at the back table at Piney Pete's, chewing slowly. It was getting late. She was running out of money, and seriously, how many Reds, Whites, and Blues can one girl eat?

"So did you want anything else?" Millicent stood over her, and Elizabeth noticed her nails were painted pink with a tiny pineapple in the center of each finger.

She shook her head and finished up her coffee in big gulps. Something about its bitter taste gave her courage. "Where's Aaron this morning?" Elizabeth finally asked.

Millicent didn't answer right away, so Elizabeth began to make tiny rips in the corner of the place mat. "Isn't he normally around?"

"Guess he's sleeping in." Millicent's smile was razor sharp.

As soon as she walked away, Elizabeth texted the two Ashleys. "Can't get a pic today. He's not here."

"Hugs" texted back Ashley two. Ashley one didn't answer. She'd been doing that a lot lately.

Across the street and down the road a little, Mrs. Herbert sat in the back of the Lost Treasures Thrift and Throwaway Store and made a phone call to Florida.

"Ma, is everything okay?" asked her daughter. "This is the third time you've called today."

"I'm fine, sweetie. Can you put Sophia on?"

"It's Dad's old store. It's getting to be too much for you. Maybe you should sell it." It was her daughter's answer to all things, but Mrs. Herbert would never sell the Lost Treasures Thrift and Throwaway Store. Never.

"No, sweetie, I'm fine. I just want to speak with my grand-daughter."

When Sophia got on the phone, Mrs. Herbert practically shouted. "Remember when you asked about the Elvis Ruby action dolls? I think I found someone who would know if they're going to be released."

At least she could do that much for Sophia. There was that rumor action figures had been made. She'd find out if the dolls were available even though Elvis Ruby was out of the show.

Perhaps she would ask Emily. Maybe that was something that Elvis would know. Maybe he had some way of finding out?

Right outside the Lost Treasures store, RJ leaned up against the wall, keeping watch. It was a perfect hiding place, close enough to get a good view of the doors of the Pancake Palace yet not close enough to be spotted. The last thing he wanted was for his sister, Elizabeth, to catch him.

Finally Elizabeth headed out the door. He could see her stepping down the side stairs, too busy texting to pay the slightest attention to where she was walking.

Now all he needed was an Elvis sighting and he was good to go.

When *TweenStar* was on, RJ had always voted for Elvis Ruby, no matter what. Even that week when Jasmeen sang that heartbreaking song and dedicated it to people whose favorite color was orange. And the week when Ramon played a solo on his bass guitar that the judges called "one for the history books," and everyone, even Elizabeth, began to say that Ramon might have a chance of winning.

Of course, now that Elvis Ruby was practically living next door and Elizabeth was the all-time best customer of the Pancake Palace, she'd probably deny she ever said such things. But RJ had never wavered. Every *TweenStar* episode, he voted for Elvis. Sometimes he even voted twice.

A guy could tell his favorite *TweenStar* that, couldn't he? If Elvis knew he was a true fan, then maybe they'd be friends. Real friends.

Maybe then Elvis would be that superstar he watched on TV instead of Aaron, the kid who mumbled, took up way too much of Cecilia's time, was afraid of water from the cedar swamp stream, and never looked him in the eye. To be perfectly honest, Aaron was kind of a loser. He hoped for more. The real Elvis Ruby had to be better.

After a while, RJ spotted someone out in the back, taking out the garbage behind the Pancake Palace. It had to be him. RJ broke into a run.

"Hey, Aaron," he shouted. "I have to tell you something."

Elvis turned around, holding the empty garbage cans.

"It's about a name," RJ shouted while he ran. "I know. I know. I know the secret." But when he got close, he stopped.

He was taller than Elvis Ruby. He'd never noticed that before. RJ was never taller than anyone. For as long as he could remember, he had always been the shortest kid in the class. Either Elvis was a lot shorter in person than he looked on TV or RJ was growing. Either way, it made him pause.

"What secret? What name?" asked Elvis, standing so much like a statue that only his lips moved.

"Crud," RJ said under his breath. He kicked at the dirt three times before he answered. "Nothing."

"You mentioned a name. You had a secret about a name," said Elvis. This time even his lips hardly moved.

"Er. Yeah. Here's the secret. It's about my name. It's not really RJ, you know. It's Robert John."

The statue moved. Elvis put down the garbage can. "It's a good name, but I like RJ better."

Friends and Secrets

When Cecilia came over later that afternoon, Elvis told her about RJ. "It was a close one. When he ran up to me and started shouting, I thought he'd found out."

She should have known that RJ would do something like this. Cecilia cut a large piece of pancake and shoved way too much of it into her mouth. "I'm so, so sorry." She chewed every last bit, swallowing hard. "He knows," she said finally.

"How?" Elvis asked.

"I told," she said softly, in almost a whisper. "He was asking me about the scrapbook, and before I knew it I was telling him everything." And like a clogged-up faucet that has finally been fixed, words poured out. "I told," she said over and over again. "I'm so, so sorry." She said that over and over again too.

Once when Storm was a puppy, he somehow managed to wriggle out of Cecilia's arms and land hard on his back. For a long time he lay there with his pudgy legs pointing up at the sky, trying to figure out how he fell so fast when only seconds before he had been in a warm safe place. Cecilia never forgot his surprised dropped-puppy look.

But she had never seen that look on a human before, until now.

"Did you tell anyone else?" Elvis asked. "Your parents?"

Cecilia shook her head.

"Uncle Frank?"

"No, of course not."

"So it's just you and RJ?" he asked, still with that surprised-puppy look.

"RJ told his mom. He didn't think moms counted."

Elvis picked up a straw and drummed a slow beat. "They count most of all."

Cecilia nodded.

"Anyone else?" he asked.

Cecilia poked her fork at the pools of maple syrup on her plate. "Elizabeth, probably. RJ never said, but it's obvious."

The door swung open. Jack Junior stormed in, carrying a toy airplane. When he tossed it into the air, it sailed across the room and smashed into the wall. Andrea and Big Jack followed fast behind him.

Before Elvis could grab some menus, Aunt Emily hurried by with a few glasses of lemonade. "I've got it." She waved for him to stay. "You sit down."

Elvis waited for the Blades to get settled and for Aunt Emily to take their orders before he spoke again. "What makes you think Elizabeth knows?"

"Remember when she went with us that day we went to the cedar swamp?"

"So?"

"That's your proof."

"Why? Maybe she wanted to go to the cedar swamp."

"With her little brother and his friends? In shoes with those heels?"

"Oh."

"And then at my birthday when she welcomed you to New Jersey."

"And what's so weird about saying 'welcome'? In every interview I had and every time I came to a new city, people said that."

"Exactly. Superstars get welcomed. Reporters say welcome because they want a story. But it's not something kids say unless"—Cecilia waved her fork—"they think they're talking to someone famous."

"Regular kids don't say that?"

She shook her head. "Look. Elizabeth is thirteen. You're

eleven. She hardly notices her own eleven-year-old brother, at least not while I'm around. If she didn't know you were Elvis Ruby, she'd treat you the same way she treats him."

The beat he drummed with his straw grew even slower. "I thought it was Aaron they liked."

"I'm sorry," she said for the twenty-seventh time.

"So they didn't buy the part about Aaron liking homework. I thought that was a nice touch."

"Me too." Cecilia nodded. "If I didn't know, you would have fooled me."

Jack Junior's plane crashed on the table, knocking over a half-empty glass of lemonade.

Elvis grabbed a wad of napkins and began wiping up. "A lot of people know," he said.

"I think they'll keep quiet." But Cecilia wasn't really certain. Ten thousand dollars was a lot of money, and people could use it in this town.

Elvis picked up the toy plane and threw it across the room. Jack Junior went running. Big Jack hurried behind him.

Elvis turned back to Cecilia and gave a sad smile. "What happens now?"

When Millicent Talks in a Soothing Voice, You Know You're in Trouble

That evening in New York City on Broadway at 8:04, curtains went up. And *TweenStar* winner Jasmeen sang and danced to a full house. She received three standing ovations.

On a stage in Baltimore, Cher received ovations too. Her father was the first one standing.

In Wares Grove, Elvis cleared the tables while the purple-striped tree frogs croaked out a symphony.

And Cecilia and her mom made brownies.

And the next morning Aunt Emily still fixed the best pancakes in the state of New Jersey. Everything seemed to be the same. Elvis wandered up and down the Pancake Palace, pouring coffee and taking orders.

"Hi, Aaron," said a woman with two little kids in tow.

At least he was still Aaron to the customers.

"We'll have a stack of Reds"—the woman pointed to herself—"a stack of Whites"—she pointed to her daughter—"and Blues"—she pointed to her son.

They were Tuesday morning regulars who lived a few towns away, but he never remembered their names. The little kids were filled with pleases and thank-yous. The mom was a big tipper. The entire family possessed an odd preference for table number seven and an undying affection for any song by Lady Gaga.

On his way back to the counter, he topped off Jacob Clayton's coffee cup.

Jacob nodded thanks and then went back to his whispery conversation with Millicent. Something he said made Millicent giggle.

Two men appeared in the doorway, covered in cobwebs.

Instead of sitting down in a booth and waiting to be served like most customers, they stood at the door, giving the place a once-over.

The first thing Elvis noticed was their cameras. They were larger than what most tourists carried. The next thing he noticed was their jeans. Fancy stitches on the back pockets meant they had spent lots of money. And there wasn't a single resident of Wares Grove who'd be caught dead in the glitzy, designer, studded belt the red-haired guy was wearing.

"Piney Pete's Pancake Palace?" said the first one. He pulled cobwebs off his camera and wiped them on his shirt.

"More like Piney Pete's Pancake Shack," the red-haired guy answered. He wandered over to an empty table and put his hands on one of the wildflowers in the mason jar. He pulled on a petal and crushed it between his fingers.

The first one took a picture of the flowers, crushed petals and all. Like a starting gun in a relay race, the camera clicked.

Elvis ducked behind the counter, ready to make a run for it. Before he could head for the door, Millicent was at his side. "Don't panic yet," she whispered. "And don't do anything stupid to draw attention to yourself like storming out the back door." The tone of her voice was soothing and calm, which could only mean one thing. She thought the situation was dangerous too.

As soon as Millicent walked over to the table, the red-haired guy complained about the cobwebs.

"Oh, I'm sorry. That's our resident spider. He lives here," said Millicent sweetly. "Didn't you see the gigantic sign?"

Aunt Emily stopped making pancakes. She ducked behind the counter and whispered, "I'll go see what I can find out. Maybe they spoke to Mrs. Herbert." If they'd stopped anyplace in town, Aunt Emily would know soon. She hurried out the back door.

"We're from *Celebrity Scoop Magazine*." The red-haired guy handed Millicent a card. "We're checking out some leads. We got a few phone calls that said Elvis Ruby was hiding out in the Pinelands. We actually got one phone call that said he was here."

Elvis gasped. Jacob Clayton let out a heavy cough. The two little kids from table seven shouted. "Elvis Ruby! Where?"

"Did you see him?" asked the red-haired guy. He pulled out a picture of Elvis and began showing it around.

"There's a huge reward," the other one added.

"No," the two kids said at the same time.

The mom at table seven added, "The only boy we ever see is the boy who pours our coffee."

The guy pulling out cobwebs turned to Millicent. "Oh, yeah. Where is he?"

Millicent shrugged. "I sent him on an errand."

Behind the counter, Elvis heard the footsteps get closer.

"Hey, did you see this kid?" The voice was right above him. They must be talking to Jacob Clayton. "There's a ten-thousand-dollar reward for the person who turns him in."

Jacob slurped his coffee. "Yeah, I've seen this boy."

"You have?" The two men, the family from table seven, and Millicent asked all at once.

"About a week or two ago," said Jacob. "About fifty miles south of here, there's a small restaurant almost like this one. Everyone mixes them up."

"But this place has better pancakes," added Millicent. She grabbed a pen and a napkin. "Here, I can draw you a map. If you make a quick turn left onto the sugar-sand road, you'll get there faster."

Elvis Gets a Bad Review

That night, Elvis waited on the front porch. As soon as heard the first note, he hurried to the back of Barnegat Al's.

Jacob sat in his usual place. Instead of a violin, he strummed a guitar. Elvis sat down next to him on the bench, waiting for Jacob to finish his song.

"What happened to your violin?" he asked.

Jacob never looked up. Instead he ran his fingers up and down the frets of the guitar. "Wasn't sure if I'd have a teacher after what happened today, Elvis." It was the first time Jacob ever called him by his real name, and it hung in the air with his angry notes. "Or Aaron. Or whatever your name is," Jacob added.

"What happened to those *Celebrity Scoop Magazine* guys?" asked Elvis.

"That shortcut that Millicent told them about did exactly what she thought it would do. Their car got buried in the sugar sand. It took me hours to tow them out, and then they headed down south to another restaurant."

"Thanks for not telling," said Elvis.

"I'm not stupid. I never bought the stuff about your abuelo for a minute. I knew you played. But how come you didn't tell me? I told you about Millicent and about the love song. I thought we were friends."

"It was a hard one to tell," said Elvis. "There was ten thousand dollars hanging on that secret."

Jacob pressed his hand to his chest and smiled. "And my secrets had to do with my heart and I shared them. Those are the secrets that matter."

"I'm sorry." It was the only thing he could think of saying.

"And what's worse is that Millicent never told me either. All that time we spent together. All those promises. And she never told. She never trusted me." Jacob played the sad, sad notes of a man whose heart was breaking.

Elvis turned to leave.

"By the way," said Jacob. "I never was an Elvis Ruby fan. Never liked his stuff."

It was the first time in his life Elvis Ruby ever got a bad

review. And it didn't sting as much as he'd thought it would. "How come?" he asked.

"His voice is great," said Jacob. "And he knows how to play. He's electric when he performs onstage."

Elvis nodded. "That's what everyone says."

"But he's a little too commercial. He plays what everyone wants to hear. And not what he feels like playing."

Jacob went back to his guitar. He strummed a whole song before he spoke again. "They're coming back, you know. We can't keep them away forever. If not those guys, then others." His notes got faster. "It's only a matter of time."

Better Than Pancakes?

Jacob was right. They'd be back. Elvis knew their tactics from before. They traveled in packs like wolves. There was never just one.

Soon it would be over.

He thought about calling his father. Maybe he could come. But in daylight? And then what? They could go on the run? He'd go back to that apartment? His father was still traveling with Cher. Her show was supposed to continue for a few more months. If he called, then that meant that Cher would have to give up her show.

"There's a guy I know. He's a little odd but he has a house so far in the Pinelands that you have to walk a mile to find it. We could hide out there. I'd stay with you," said Millicent.

But Elvis shook his head.

It would just put it off. For a few days maybe. Another month? Too many people knew who he was.

Aaron, the boy he had pretended to be, was fading away fast. He'd have to think of something.

The next day he ached from thinking about it . . .

That afternoon during lunch, when three teenage boys and their parents sat at table number three, he grumbled.

"Oh, look," the mother said to her sons, "they have cranberry pancakes."

And it made him grumble more.

Teenage boys were always good for second servings, especially if Millicent was waiting on them. If the taste of Piney Pete's Reds and Blues didn't tempt them, she'd give them a long smile and they'd order up another stack.

But before the family finished up their first pile of pancakes, Elvis put on a symphony with bleak hollow notes and shattering cymbals.

When Millicent asked them if they wanted seconds, they all refused. They left the Pancake Palace with pancakes still on their plates.

"First time that's ever happened," said Aunt Emily. "Do you think it was a bad batch?"

A group of hikers came in, tired from the sun and worn out from trudging through the sugar sand.

"You all look like you could use a cup of free coffee or maybe some lemonade," said Aunt Emily.

The hikers sipped gratefully.

The song Elvis played next could only be described as chilling. It was the type of tune that would make you want to zip up your sweatshirt, rub your hands together for warmth, and wonder if there was a draft someplace. One by one, the hikers drifted out the door.

Aunt Emily hurried into the back room to make a new batch of pancakes. She stirred in the eggs with great tenderness and checked the grill for the perfect temperature. Her next batch would be light and fluffy, with exactly the right amount of chewiness. Even more perfect than her regular ones.

For the next few hours it didn't matter who stopped by. Tourists. Regular customers. The busload of senior citizens from the retirement community. The couple who got lost on their way to Atlantic City. Elvis wanted them out. He chose his music carefully. Each song was especially designed to be grating and annoying, like insect bites.

And the customers began to leave.

"Hey, free pancakes here." But this time it wasn't Aunt Emily pushing the plate around. It was Millicent.

"Cut it out," she said. "What are you doing? They're not lingering. Rule number one of keeping a restaurant in business is don't chase away the paying customers."

Aunt Emily hurried out from the kitchen, her spatula in her hand. "What's going on here?"

"It seems," said Millicent, "I've created a monster."

Elvis was ready to stop anyway. His experiment was done.

Aunt Emily's pancakes were the most mouthwatering treats in the entire state of New Jersey, but the songs drove the customers away.

In the contest between food and music, the choice was clear. Music won.

Music beat everything.

But then there was a cough. Elvis glanced around the room.

Way back in the two-seater Cecilia sat, tapping her feet in her odd way. He hadn't noticed her before. She must have come in when he was racing back and forth, changing songs.

So music didn't beat everything, thought Elvis. No matter what he played, Cecilia was there.

He hurried toward her.

"What's happening here?" she asked. "Are you okay?"

When he didn't answer, Cecilia poked him in the arm. "We're friends, aren't we? You'd tell me if you weren't okay? Friends tell each other that kind of stuff. Right?"

She tried to poke him again, but Elvis grabbed her hand.

"Yes," he whispered. "Friends tell."

Aaron's Goodbye

Later that night Aaron waited in his room. He gave Fred a last hug.

Then Elvis Ruby snuck out the back door and went into the night.

Elvis Ruby's Secret

For a small dog, Storm had a loud bark. It sounded almost ferocious if you were standing outside Cecilia's bedroom window late at night like Elvis was. He circled around the house a few times, but he could hear Storm following his every move, chasing him with those barks. Finally Elvis stood in front of the open window. "Cecilia," he whispered loudly.

"What's going on?" Cecilia peeked out the window with Storm in her arms. As soon as the dog spotted Elvis, he growled.

Elvis took a few steps back. "I don't think he likes me."

"Don't be silly. He likes everyone," said Cecilia, but when Elvis moved closer to the house, Storm showed his teeth.

Elvis waved the old violin over the top of his head. "Come on. Let's go."

"I knew it," Cecilia shouted. "I knew you'd come through."
When she climbed out the window without him, Storm's
barks turned into whimpers.

The air was chilly, especially for spring. Elvis could see his
breath as they hurried across the yard. They hadn't even
reached the sugar-sand path when Elvis started talking. "You
know what I'm most famous for? Messing up. Elvis Ruby the
musician sold magazines, but Elvis Ruby the kid who disappointed an entire television viewing audience sold millions."

Elvis told Cecilia about that night on *TweenStar*. "There
was only a handful of contestants left. We were all supposed
to sing Elvis Presley songs." He told how his friend Ramon
wore a 1950s-style leather jacket with his hair slicked back.
"He looked good." Jasmeen was dressed in the black-and-
white striped prisoner's uniform, all ready to belt out the song
"Jailhouse Rock." Another contestant wore a white Las Vegas–
style jumpsuit, complete with bell-bottoms and sparkles on
the lapels. Elvis wasn't dressed like any of them. His father
had a plan. "Let the others dress up like Elvis Presley, you keep
it simple. That's how you'll stand out," his father had said.

So Elvis Ruby wore his jeans and a T-shirt. His father was
right. He did stand out.

He was named for Elvis Presley after all.

"We expect big things from you," the *TweenStar* judges had said.

"Big things," a reporter from *Celebrity Scoop Magazine* had written.

"Big things," his father agreed.

"You must have been under so much pressure," said Cecilia.

Elvis took a few long steps before he spoke again. "For the first time in my life, I was really nervous."

Cecilia nodded, urging him on.

"That's when Zander Fox, the host of *TweenStar*, saw me backstage, pulled me aside and gave me a pep talk. He told me I was a sure thing. That I could never lose."

"That was nice," Cecilia said. "He thought you could win."

Elvis picked up a pebble and threw it into the fishpond. Cecilia took a few more steps before she noticed he wasn't right behind her. She turned around.

"No. That's not what Zander meant," Elvis said. "He told me there was a schedule they had to keep. They had a Broadway show to produce, and that *TweenStar* action figure made in the winner's likeness isn't something they can rush. Zander said the audience doesn't always pick the contestant with the most money-making abilities. After a few bad seasons, the *TweenStar* producers decided they couldn't leave the results to chance. Zander said it didn't matter because I would have probably won anyway if the audience's votes counted."

"Wait. Are you saying that the whole *TweenStar* show was fixed?"

Elvis nodded. "It was all a fraud. My friend Ramon didn't have a chance. None of the other contestants did. No matter how bad I was, I was going to be the winner."

"So you froze?"

"Not right away. I remember waiting on the stage and for some weird reason all I could think about was *TweenStar* and what a dumb name it is for a contest. It's the 'tween' part that's stupid. It's a word grownups use. No kid I know would ever call himself that. So the spotlight goes on and I'm standing there in front of millions of people who are waiting for me to sing 'Heartbreak Hotel,' and I can't because I'm thinking about the show's producers and their really rotten name choice. That's crazy, right? To think of something like that? I mean . . . I should have been singing. I should have done what they wanted."

"But you couldn't," said Cecilia. "It wasn't what *you* wanted."

"I wanted to win, but not like that," said Elvis, and the heavy breath he took curled in the air and floated toward the sky. "I think I squeaked out a note or two. That's when someone in the audience laughed."

"People always laugh at wrong notes." Cecilia shook her head. "I hate it when they laugh."

The ground shook. There was a rumbling sound.

Cecilia and Elvis ducked behind some trees.

"Look." Cecilia pointed at the parade of trucks and vans coming down the road. Each one had a television station logo painted on its side. One by one, they parked. First in front of the Pancake Palace, then in front of the Lost Treasures Thrift and Throwaway Store. Then Barnegat Al's and the Wares Grove Hunt Club. When they used up all the parking spaces, the trucks parked on the lawns and the gardens.

Cameras clicked, spotlights appeared, and the night grew brighter.

Like wildfire the paparazzi were moving across Wares Grove. They trampled on the sugar sand. They stomped on flowers. That goofy blond-haired guy from the television show *TMI* stood with a camera right on the front lawn of the Old Church.

"They found me," said Elvis.

"Not yet. They're not coming toward us. They're all heading to the Pancake Palace." Cecilia pulled him toward the woods. "Let's go."

The Poor Devil

On a different spring night at a different time the Jersey
Devil wandered near the bank of a stream and there was
Sammy Buck sitting on a fallen log. Years had passed. Sammy
was older now, with tufts of gray hair and an old man's voice
that trembled when he talked, but he still had a fiddle in one
hand and his bow in the other.

"Well, look at you," said Sammy Buck when the Devil said
hello. "Didn't know it was possible for you to look any worse,
but you look more devilish than I remembered."

The Jersey Devil spent the next hour or so telling Sammy
Buck about the unfairness of the world and all the horrible
names he'd been called. He even pulled a crumpled-up article

from the local paper that he had wrapped around his horn and waved it in front of Sammy Buck's face.

Then the Devil pointed to the fiddle and asked about the song. He told Sammy how he had searched the woods, tree by tree by tree, and sifted through each grain of sand.

"It's been over forty years now since I last saw you and all that time you've been looking?" asked Sammy Buck. "I told you the last time, you might as well give up."

The Jersey Devil stomped his hooves and kicked over a pitch pine tree. If Sammy Buck were a lesser man, he might have been scared. Instead he looked the Devil in the eye. "It might do you some good to ask me why?"

And even though the Devil never asked, Sammy Buck spoke in his trembling old man's voice and he told the Jersey Devil the secret to the song. "When you're so busy trying to be what other people think you should be, you'll never find your own music."

The Jersey Devil hugged himself with his great bat wings, glanced down at his long tail and cloven feet, and looked at what he had become. Then he let out a hideous roar and flew into the trees.

Sammy Buck put his fiddle to his chin and played his own song.

Unexpected Beats

Somehow Cecilia managed to find her way to the cedar swamp stream. There were a few wrong turns and Elvis stepped in the path of a quite harmless garden snake, but they made it.

Cecilia had never been here at night. The trees loomed overhead. The red waters were dark and inky.

Elvis was standing a little too close to the stream, and Cecilia wondered if she should shout out a warning. He was leaning over a large tree stump, examining it with his flashlight.

"Hey, there's writing here." He waved her over. "It says your name."

Cecilia bent down and traced the letters with her fingers. She could feel the graceful curves of the *C* and the loopy way the *I* ran into the other letters. She knew the handwriting.

"My mother carved this a few days after I was born to mark the spot." She stood up and looked around again. "I guess that means we're in the right place."

Elvis placed the violin under his chin and then picked up the bow. "Ready?" he asked.

Cecilia nodded.

But he stopped when his bow touched the strings.

"What's wrong?" she asked. "Are you still afraid to play?"

Elvis shook his head. "No. I'm good. I don't know how I know it. But I'm good. Once I let out that secret, there was room for the music. But I want you to do it with me."

Cecilia shook her head. "We've been through this before. I can't."

"But it's your song. If this place is going to sing, well then I'd think it would want to hear from you."

"No."

"Have you ever tried?"

"To sing? Many times."

Elvis poked her playfully with the bow. "You know, fifteen million people would kill for a chance to do a duet with Elvis Ruby during his comeback number."

He was joking and she knew it. "I don't know any songs. I'm not musical. It's not something I can do." She touched his arm. "Please play."

"You don't need to know songs. Make it up. That's what I do sometimes."

"But what if . . ."

"Don't even say it. Who's gonna laugh?"

She closed her eyes. It would be better if she didn't see him watching her.

And Cecilia sang.

She sang about a girl who took lonely bus rides to school and ate lunch by herself and lost bunny slippers when she wandered at night. It was a slow, sad beat, and a happy beat. It was off-key and on key, sometimes occurring all at once in a single note.

He accompanied her with the violin and sang harmony to a song that had no melody.

They sang together, his voice perfect and clear, her voice loud and out of tune.

The song ended with a high note, then a low note, then suddenly without a flourish or warning.

When it was over, she opened her eyes.

He was smiling. "We did it." He waved his violin. "And I was able to play. After all this time. No problems at all. And you sang. You said you couldn't do it but you did." He pointed his bow at her. "You know what you are? You are syncopated."

Elvis Ruby had called her syncopated.

They had played their song. There was nothing to do now but to see if the Pinelands would answer.

A Different Kind of Tune

They waited.

There were night birds and insects. There was the rustle of the wind.

In the distance a coyote howled.

"Do you hear it?" she asked.

Elvis shook his head. "Where's it supposed to come from?"

"The air. My parents said it was in the air."

They listened more.

"Should I play again?" he asked.

Something moved nearby. The trees shook.

"I found them," said a voice in the darkness, one that was filled with relief.

It was Cecilia's mom.

Mrs. Wreel grabbed Cecilia tight. "You had us so scared." She shouted back into the woods, "They're here!"

There were more rustles. Millicent and Jacob stepped out of the darkness. Behind them were Elizabeth and RJ.

"Storm wouldn't stop barking. That's how I found out you were gone," explained Mrs. Wreel. "Your father is off searching in another direction. I need to call him on my cell."

"And you know what's happening at the Pancake Palace, right?" asked Millicent. "My mom kept them busy so we could sneak out. She's probably making pancakes for everyone, but I'm sure some of the paparazzi are on their way. They probably heard the . . . er . . . song you played."

"Why are you here anyway?" asked Elizabeth.

"Waiting for the pine trees to sing," explained Elvis.

"Oh that," said RJ. "We know the story."

But when Elvis played a little more, RJ listened to the trees.

"I don't hear it," said Elizabeth.

"Me neither," said Millicent.

They turned to Elvis.

He shook his head.

Cecilia sighed. "So there was never a song. All this time I searched for nothing."

Mrs. Wreel had finished her phone call and now she cleared her throat. "No. You were right, Cecilia. I heard it the day you were born. We'll have to talk later. I think my theory about endorphins and happiness was wrong."

After a while, Elizabeth and RJ were shouting out requests and Jacob was singing along. While the others listened to Elvis play, Cecilia and her mom went to sit near the stump that had her name carved in it. "I've been thinking about this since we spoke. I have another theory," Mrs. Wreel explained. "I was happy today, crazy happy to see you safe, and there was no music from the pines. And I'm crazy happy on most days just to have you as my daughter, and I don't hear anything. Maybe what happened that night you were born was something more. The night you were born the Pinelands sang." Mrs. Wreel gave Cecilia a squeeze. "That song played just for you."

More people were gathering. Word was getting out that Elvis Ruby was here. They all moved to a clearing in the woods. Flashlights shone like spotlights. Paparazzi cameras flashed.

Instead of running, Elvis stood on the stump of a tree. "My name is Elvis *Aaron* Ruby," he shouted to the crowd. "I can rock. And rap. And my drumming has been called 'explosive.' And I can make a piano talk in seven different languages. And when I sing, I'll make you think of memories you haven't had yet."

The crowd screamed.

"And I also make a mean blueberry pancake," he added.

This time when the crowd cheered, Millicent's voice was the loudest.

Then he picked up his violin and Elvis played.

Cecilia stood near a tree and watched the crowd sway and clap and tap their feet. She swayed and clapped and tapped at the wrong beats in the wrong time in the wrong ways.

Her mother put a hand on Cecilia's shoulder. "I'm sorry, sweetie. I'm sorry you came all this way and never heard your song."

Cecilia took her mother's hand. She *had* heard her song. She had sung it with her friend.

It was loud and off-key. Unexpected. Syncopated.

Cecilia closed her eyes.

And in the Pinelands there was music.

The end.

Epilogue: The Small Matter of the Ten Thousand Dollars

In the Pinelands, they say the trees will keep your secrets. People, on the other hand, are a different story.

The reporter who takes the calls for *Celebrity Scoop Magazine* will tell you all about it. He got thousands of calls telling him the whereabouts of Elvis Ruby. He narrowed it down to three pretty good leads.

There were 157 calls from people claiming they saw Elvis Ruby eating curly fries in a restaurant in Tulsa, Oklahoma. But 314 people claimed that he was working in a logging camp in Alaska. And over 714 said he was somewhere in the Pinelands of New Jersey.

The reporter from *Celebrity Scoop Magazine* sent his paparazzi to all three places. When you're in the celebrity-spotting business, you get a lot of false leads.

How'd he find him in New Jersey so fast? It wasn't hard.

Elizabeth's friend Ashley told. Not the second Ashley, she didn't tell anyone because best friends keep secrets, right? But that first Ashley had a major crush on her seventeen-year-old brother's friend Ryan. A few days after she found out about Elvis Ruby, her brother and Ryan were playing basketball. She thought it would make Ryan pay attention to her if she told him. It didn't.

Ryan made one of the first calls to *Celebrity Scoop* and then he texted all his friends. And some of those friends told their friends who told other friends. It grew from there. At least Ashley number one learned a valuable lesson in this whole thing: Never be taken in by a boy with a good smile and a well-placed tattoo.

Mrs. Herbert never told, not even her granddaughter, Sophia. But when it was all over, she took a special trip to Florida, and over pancakes (ones that were nowhere near as good as Aunt Emily's) she told Sophia all about it. She never did find out about those Elvis Ruby dolls. If you see one, buy it. It could be a collector's item someday.

RJ's mom blurted it out to her entire book club. She didn't mean to. She's chatty like RJ. And besides, they were book people. And everyone knows that book people are kind and virtuous. She didn't think they counted. Some of the book people were virtuous. They kept it to themselves. And some told their friends who told their friends who told their friends. And some called *Celebrity Scoop Magazine*.

Remember Amanda, that former *TweenStar* contestant who became friends with Cher during the traveling show of *The Sound of Music*? She mentioned it to her parents. Forget *Celebrity Scoop Magazine*, her mom immediately telephoned the producers of *TweenStar*. They're still in negotiations. Right now it looks like if Amanda reveals everything that Cher told her about what happened to Elvis Ruby those weeks he went missing, she'll get one more chance to be a contestant in the next season of *TweenStar*.

Those two rude kayakers, the ones who left a fifty, called *Celebrity Scoop* too. It's a funny thing, since they both promised they'd make the call together, but neither waited for the other.

The boy with the Elvis Ruby haircut at Albert Music Hall Pickin' Shed made a call. All totaled, there were fifty-seven calls made by people with Elvis Ruby haircuts.

But the ten-thousand-dollar reward for the first call and the most complete information went to Andrea and Jack Blades. They were *TweenStar* fans and regulars at the Pancake Palace, so they suspected almost right away. That day when Elvis waved hi to them in the music hall, they were certain. It wasn't an easy decision for them. They spent an entire anxious night talking it over. In the end, they decided they needed the money for Jack Junior's education. After all, Jack Junior was a very special boy, loaded with charisma. It would be a shame to waste his talents.

Acknowledgments

If I could sing . . .

I'd sing songs of thanks to my editor, Nancy Mercado, for her guidance, patience, and faith—and for all those conversations. Her questions and insights helped me find my characters' voices. I continue to learn so much from her.

For the team at Roaring Brook who worked on this book, including Karla Reganold for her careful copy edits and John Hendrix for the incredible cover art.

I'd sing additional songs of thanks to my amazing agent, Rosemary Stimola, for believing in my writing, for being a calm voice of reason, and for always *always* being a quick email away.

For my friends and colleagues at the Ocean County Library, especially the ones in TRIS. Thanks for your incredible support and encouragement.

For Angela Zebrowski for showing me pictures of her pine trees and telling me their names.

For Elizabeth Cronin for showing me the books about the Pinelands before I even moved here on that very first library tour.

For Marguerite Dugas for sharing her research on the Jersey Devil.

For Carol Zsiga for putting that book of Pineland folklore on my desk with the page opened to the legend of the Fiddler Sammy Buck and for making sure I knew there was music in the Pines.

For Frank Domenico Cipriani and Katie Schoeneberg, who talked about the Pinelands in such vivid detail that I felt like I was walking those sugar-sand paths with them.

Thanks to those who shared their love of music: Andrew Sarnoff, Ritch Robinson, and the people at the Albert Music Hall in Waretown.

For my writing buddies / critique partners, especially C. Lee McKenzie, Jane Quaglin, Rob Robinson, Kate Lallier, and Katia Raina. Thanks for all your support, cups of tea, advice, and late-night reads.

For Marie-Andree Lebrum, Isabelle Peretz, Lauren Stewart, and Anne Barker for answering my questions about amusia in children. Thank you for lending your expertise and insights and for helping me understand the character of Cecilia. I hope I got it right.

For Stan Zebrowski for answering my questions about children overcoming stage trauma. On behalf of the character Elvis, thank you. Thank you very much.

Last but not least, for my family and friends and for my husband, Sal, who never seems to mind when I sing loud and off-key.